good deed rain

The apartment was on the corner of Holly Street, across from the bank. Jones made it there in good time and went around back and took the rickety metal stairway up. He wanted some answers. There was no breeze. His bike waited for him on the ground. His noble steed. So much depends upon a red bicycle smudged with sunlight beside the rusted fire escape.

JONES JR.

JONES JR. © 2024
Allen Frost, Good Deed Rain
Bellingham, Washington
ISBN: 979-8-3302-8508-2

Writing: Allen Frost
Cover & Illustrations: Aaron Gunderson
Cover Production: Zane Rupp
Quote: Stephen King, *Los Angeles Review of Books*, October 25, 2011.
Apple: TFK!

"Writers are actually supposed to be secret agents and we go along and see stuff and kind of record it."

—Stephen King

JONES JR.

Allen Frost

Good Deed Rain ◊ Bellingham, Washington ◊ 2024

CHAPTERS

This is Jones Junior 19
The Shoeshiner Proxy 26
Here in Avalon 31
The Broadway Incident 35
Underworld Infinity 42
Selling Avalon 47
Confessions of a Pawn Shop 52
Appointment with a Mummy 55
The Cleopatra Drift 60
X-Ray Spectacles 64
6 PM on Channel 12 70
The Paraffin Test 76
Ten-Gallon Heist 82
Submarine Telephone Booth 86
Violet Zen 92

Leandro Hiphenou	98
A Star in the Blue	102
Phil the Gorilla	106
Shakedown on Sunnyside	112
The Crimson Topaz	115
Jones the Mammoth	123
Moon Technology	129
Paradise Cove	134
Smugglers at Midnight	140
Nebraska Postcard	146
Sphinx at the Window	148
Counterfeit Atmosphere	153
The Chloroform Affair	159
Inspector Canary	165
Dreaming of Avalon	169

INTRODUCTION

Here's a strange story. It's probably the wrong way to start, I know that, but I'm going to tell it anyway: here's what I remember about JR. He was new in school, mousy, thin and small, wearing a brown t-shirt, jeans, long hair, and when the teacher introduced him to the 4th grade class, she wanted to know what his name really was. Nobody was named "JR." He insisted that was his name but she hounded him and although her interrogation got nowhere, it created a cloud in the room that everyone could feel. He was alone.

The kids in class could sense that he was a wild animal and when the last bell rang and everyone was let outside he was chased off the playground, across the street. He ran but half the class was after him. There was a lot of shouting and saying his name the way you'd buzz a kazoo. He couldn't escape, they kept coming for him. Wrestled down into the leaves on the hill. There were boys around him pushing him and some of them were punching too. Not to say I tried to stop them. I watched it from a distance, but I remembered it all these years.

Well, fine. He moved around a lot as a kid. His first day in a school would always be a trial. We don't know what happened to him, we lost track long ago. But maybe he became Jones Jr. If the 1970s stood still, and America never grew out of the loud age of petroleum. There was a time when it seemed like the 1970s was reality. If you were there you know what I mean, or maybe you only see it on TV where it still lives in fading movies and detective shows.

—AF, May 18, 2024

THIS IS JONES JUNIOR

The phone began to ring.

It rang once and waited a moment and rang again.

And again.

It was like breathing.

On the fourth ring, the answering machine picked up, "This is Jones Junior. At the tone leave your name and message. I'll get back to you."

"JJ, this is Phil. I need your help…Are you there? You must be…C'mon, get up, I need to talk to you…" The voice in the telephone paused, but there was a rasp indicating Phil was still there, inhaling and exhaling and waiting impatiently. "Jones! Wake up!"

That was all the message the machine could record. It held enough time for a poem. The line went dead, the trailer was quiet again, but Jones Jr. knew it would ring again. He got out of bed and headed for the phone. He knew Phil was already dialing. Sure enough, as he reached for the receiver the telephone rang. He lifted it and croaked, "Yeah."

"I need a favor."

Jones glanced at the clock. "It's 7:48. A.M. It's not even 8."

"I appreciate that information, Jones, but I got a problem. I can't make it to work."

"And—"

"And I need you to cover for me, J."

Jones groaned.

"Listen, JJ this is important, my parole officer is checking on me today and if I'm not there, she's—"

"You want me to impersonate you in front of a cop?"

"She don't even know what I look like! The station sends her to make sure I'm doing the job they got me. Just pretend to be me, that's all you have to do."

"I do have a job of my own, you know, Phil."

"Do you?"

"Yes. I mean…not at this very moment…"

"Come on, Jones!"

"I'm on standby. I'm awaiting orders."

"Okay, okay, I hate to do this but I'm going to bring something up. It's something you'd like to forget. You probably don't remember the time I saved your life."

Jones remembered.

So he agreed to do Phil's job for the day. "What is it anyway?"

Phil told him, and was quick to add, "Don't worry, most of the time you're just sitting there. You can listen to the radio. There's a Dodgers game. I keep my grip in a locker." He told him the combination.

"I'll do it Phil, but I don't want to hear about this debt I owe you ever again."

"You won't, I promise. We're even now, J. This time you saved my life."

"Yeah, alright." Jones hung up. He didn't have time to make coffee, but he figured he could get some at the station. It didn't take him long to get ready and out the door. A seagull ran from the sound of the tin slam. "Sorry," Jones said, "no breakfast today." No toast, no crust to throw. On the parking lot twenty feet away, the seagull glared at him. These were strange birds, ghost birds, if you live by the sea they will watch you. Jones tried to do right by them.

He took hold of his bicycle and led it from the trailer. A red Schwinn 3-speed. It was no Lincoln Continental. He missed his car. Especially when it rained. He didn't need reminding what a simple luxury it was to open a door and sit behind a wheel, as he heaved himself onto the bike seat and steadied himself before launch. The gull audience screeched and chuckled and weaved overhead.

Jones wrecked his car in a car chase. Actually, it wasn't much of a chase. He wanted it to be one of those Hollywood thrills, with loud music and his big car roaring over hills, airborne, but he drove into a one-way street and went up over a curb and hit a brick wall.

Now he rode a bike.

Even in first gear it wasn't easy to pedal. The tires needed air.

He wobbled away from the sound of the ocean across the asphalt dusted with sand. The trailer was parked against a hill with a view of the water and a fine view of the parking lot. Jones couldn't complain—it was usually only millionaires this close to the sea—and he had it for free. All he needed to do was keep an eye on the lot. Keep the hooligans away at night, clean up whatever the beachgoers left behind. He raked the path to the water so it resembled a Zen garden.

He had another job too, one that paid. He had to make money somehow.

He was a private detective.

The entrance to the parking lot was secured by a heavy rusted chain. In the middle of the sway hung a padlock that could have secured Davy Jones' locker. No relation. Jones stopped his bike and stepped off. His white sneakers slapped the paving. He got a copper key from his pocket and fumbled with the lock until it creaked apart.

A station wagon was waiting to enter. The driver wore a straw hat. After Jones cleared the chains to the side, the driver tipped the hat. Jones could see a fishing pole leaning in the back of the car like bamboo. Sometimes people on foot would sneak in early to fish and that was alright by Jones. He didn't guard the beach or the sea, just a parking lot.

It was already a beautiful spring morning. His faded yellow suit shone with sunlight and a nice breeze pushed at his back. He had to stand on the pedals to get the bike going, turning onto the road. Once he got out of first gear, he reached forward into the flowered basket between the handlebars and took out a walkie-talkie. The road was smooth enough he could keep steering with one hand. The car crash happened months ago, he had plenty of time to practice the skill. He switched the radio on and said, "You there, Roscoe?"

After a moment, a mechanical voice answered, "You forgot to say, Over."

Jones pressed the red button again, "Okay, sorry. My mistake. Give me a call if you hear anything. Over."

"Roger. Over and out."

Jones leaned ahead and dropped the radio back into the basket. Back in the trailer, Roscoe listened to the police scanner. If something sounded interesting, he would let Jones know. That's how Jones got most of his cases. He'd show up at the scene of the crime and offer a helping hand. $200 a day, plus expenses.

Traffic was light this morning. It could be a problem later on when tempers rose with the temperature. A fat man riding a bike on the roadside could attract some unwanted attention. Cars would stack up behind him and wait to pass him and sometimes they yelled at him as they roared around. Not everyone. People were generally kind, nothing to worry about, it was all in the game, and Jones had been in it long enough to know it was those few unkind types who ended up on the police radio.

It was a mile ride into town, a little further to the bus station.

THE SHOESHINER PROXY

A Greyhound was parked, rumbling and clouding diesel. Jones rode through the fog that formed along the curb. If he got on, he'd go two hours north. He wouldn't have willingly got on the bus, why would he? But he would be on it, he just didn't know that yet.

He walked the bike into the station and steered it towards the lockers. Some uniformed people, some sort of club or secret order that wore orange suits, were taking up four benches. A woman with what looked like a possum in a cage was watching him. The shoeshine stand was next to a couple vending machines. A man was getting instant coffee from one. Jones felt too hot for coffee, something cold would be better. He wondered if they had Moxie.

The lockers were set in an alcove stacked like a bee's honeycomb. Phil told Jones the number and the combination. Phil's grip was in there, the tools of his trade, brushes, cloth, boot polish. Jones thought about the people in orange suits, what if they wanted shines? What a way to start the day with thirty pairs of shoes.

Jones stopped when he found the locker and the kickstand stuck the bike to the floor. The combination worked. He lifted out the brown leather bag. It wasn't as heavy as he thought it would be. What if it was empty except for a treasure map Phil needed him to hide from his enemies? Jones would be dragged into a scenario he had no wish to be in.

Fortunately, that wasn't it. The bag held a couple wooden brushes, one was cracked and taped, a crusted rag, a tin of polish that Jones would find was mostly empty. Phil didn't go out of his way to impress the parole officer. It looked like something dumped out of a vacuum cleaner...except for a small transistor radio tucked in the corner, so he could listen to the Dodgers.

Phil never missed a game. He played the ponies too. It wouldn't surprise Jones to know why Phil really needed the day off—a couple of guys were looking for him.

Out in the lobby, the speaker echoed, "Pasadena, loading at Gate 3."

Jones would be on it soon. Without a ticket.

He took the bag and rolled his bike around onto the lobby tiles and parked it between a soda machine and the shoeshine stand. He dropped the bag on the chair. He never shined a shoe in his life. He wore sneakers. How hard could it be though?

The circus would have a barker to drum up business. It was just after eight in the morning, it seemed a little early for a 'Step right up!' routine. Jones stood in front of the chair staring at the lobby. All those orange suits were connected to white wingtips. If he could get one of them interested, they would all flock around him like doves.

It might have been entertaining to see Jones try.

As it turned out, after another announcement for Gate 3, they stood up and headed for their bus. Jones watched them leave. He was glad he was a detective with his own hours, not some poor slob tied to an 8-5 job, with bosses or parole officers keeping track. Plus, he was no good at this kind of work.

Someone stopped to admire his bicycle and laughed wheezily. "Nice wheels."

Jones didn't let it bother him, he heard a lot worse, he let it slide. "You want a shoeshine?"

"No way, man."

Jones shrugged. He made room next to the bag to sit down. The throne was a postcard view of the bus station. Jones could turn it over and write, "Having a wonderful time. Wish you were here." The big windows looked out on the traffic. A black car stopped and two men in black suits got out.

Jones watched them. It beat staring at the arrivals board. They crossed the floor headed for Jones. They walked like cops. Undercover.

"Are you Phil Ticks?"

Parole officers, Jones guessed. Didn't Phil say to expect a woman though? "Yeah," Jones lied, "I'm Phil."

"Put down your bag, you're coming with us."

Jones didn't even realize he was holding the

grip. "I can't leave my work. What are you? Cops?"

They weren't in the talking mood. They took hold of Jones, one on each side of him.

"Who are you guys?" Jones persisted. Something wasn't right. "Okay, let me level with you. I'm not Phil Ticks. Look, I'll show you my ID." He patted his yellow suit pocket. He left his wallet in his raincoat.

They walked Jones away from the shoeshine stand, across the tiles, the empty benches where the orange suits were, past the ticket counter towards Gate 3. Jones felt he could have raised his feet off the floor and floated. Then he felt the sharp bite of a needle through his yellow sleeve. They stood him next to the bus. The driver was busy helping someone up the stairs. Jones felt himself turning into a cloud, one of those big fluffy ones that sit on the horizon far out at sea, in the dark in the starlight. The cloud was raised and tossed into the cargo hold of the bus and covered over with bags.

HERE IN AVALON

"What are you doing here in Avalon?"

"I don't know," Jones said. He wasn't in the dark cargo bay of a Greyhound bus, not that he was aware of, he was lying down in a field.

"You're new here, aren't you?" she asked. She was so fair, Jones sat up. He wanted to talk with her. For a long time.

Another voice interceded, "Never mind, Frida. He's expected. Hello, Mr. Ticks, welcome to Avalon."

Even in this other world, Jones was still mistaken for Phil. It didn't matter to Jones. Everything around him was beautiful. Like spring unwrapped in a flower shop. He took a deep breath. It wasn't like the city where you learned not to do that. A wide grassy field with dandelions, a valley between big trees ringing it. As he stood, it was so easy, he must have been fifty pounds lighter, he felt he could have kept going up, like a balloon. "Wow…"

"You like it here?"

It was beautiful, yes, but there was also something familiar and not familiar. He couldn't quite concentrate. "Where is this place?"

"Oh, you won't find it on a map." The man thought that was funny.

"Why am I here?"

"Until you return what you took from us, we're keeping an eye on you, Mr. Ticks."

"Hold on," Jones said. "I'm not sure—"

"Of course you're not sure of a lot of things at this point. Don't worry, Frida will tell you all about it. Frida?"

She returned like a cloud and smiled. "We can take your car." She pointed.

There it was! Pale blue, parked in the field like a cow. Jones' Lincoln Continental. He laughed. He was behind the wheel. Time moved differently in Avalon. It felt great to be steering his old car again. The grass bent and swished beside them like water against the hull of a motorboat. "I don't know where I'm going," he grinned.

Frida sat in the cushioned passenger seat. "We don't need roads in Avalon, just drive past those trees to the ocean."

Suddenly they were on a beach, Jones was driving fast along the wet sand close to where the surf broke. Who knows how many times he saw this scene happen in movies and TV. Every good detective got a chance. Sometimes it was part of a car chase. Not this ride, just seagulls getting out of the way. The beach was almost exactly like the one he lived near, he walked it enough to know his trailer was just ahead, by the cliff. What was he supposed to do, just park below and hope the waves didn't wash the car away? He didn't have to worry.

The car stopped on the parking lot.

Jones knew where he was supposed to be, but his trailer wasn't slumped in the windshield view. In its place was a beach house with a deck and two chairs for watching the sea and the sunset.

"This is strange…This isn't right, I mean it's better, everything is better."

"You're not Phil Ticks, are you?" Frida said.

"No. No, my name is—"

"I know who you are," she interrupted him. She pointed at the painted sign on the picket fence.

He read aloud, "Jones Jr. Detective."

"A sneak preview of Avalon," she smiled. She was still beautiful. "This will be here for you later, you're not ready for it now. You'll have to go back." She clasped her hands. "I'll try to explain. These mistakes happen sometimes. Those two at the bus station were supposed to get Phil Ticks. He's got the box. Nobody steals from Avalon. His time is up. You got in the way, mistaken identity." She touched his hand and repeated, "You have to go back."

Jones didn't want to. He liked it here. "Wait, I don't understand. Can't we wait a little, do I have to leave right away? It's nice here. I like being with you too." He wished it, and they were sitting at the table outside the house, with a bottle of cold Moxie for each of them.

"No, Jones." They were back in the car. "You're going to wake up now."

And he did.

THE BROADWAY INCIDENT

A duffel bag was squashing him, a suitcase shoved at his feet. "What's going on in there?" a man demanded.

Jones could see daylight around the pile of bags he lay behind. "I'm here," Jones said.

The duffel was pulled away and the bus driver could see him. "A stowaway!"

"No." Jones squirmed over the metal flooring. He could remember, "Two guys knocked me out and threw me in here."

The driver slid a cowhide suitcase aside. "Stowaway, shanghai, what do I care? You don't have a ticket, you don't get to ride!" He grabbed Jones' suit and yanked him into the sunshine.

Jones held his sore arm. "Thanks. I don't want to make any trouble."

"Darn right. Not on my bus."

Jones nodded and straightened his crumpled suit as he drifted from the bus.

"Get a job!" The driver yelled at his back, "Buy a ticket like everyone else."

Gate 3 opened into the lobby again. Jones rubbed his arm. Did something bite him in the dark? Were they shipping a box of tarantulas to a zoo?

The bus station looked like no time had passed. Jones remembered being in a field.

A speaker squawked, "Pasadena bus, now departing at Gate 3."

The shoeshine stand was still where he left it. The grip too, also his bike. It wasn't a garage sale. It was time to go to work. He reached in the grip and got the stained rag and tried to give it a wave like a shipwrecked sailor, but the cloth was stiff with caked polish and flat as a vinyl LP. He considered calling out, "Shoeshines!" but that approach didn't feel right. If someone wanted clean shoes they would find him. Maybe it was finally time to visit the vending machine for a coffee. He dug in his pocket for change.

"Are you Phil Ticks?"

Jones forgot about the coffee. The coins slipped through his fingers. He was staring at two men, not the same ones that caused trouble before, but they could have been brothers. "Are you cops?"

"Not hardly," said one.

"I said, are you Phil Ticks?" said the other.

"Oh sure," Jones replied. "That's me to a tee."

"Suits me to a tee too, pal."

"Come with us," said Not Hardly.

"What? Why?"

Mr. Tee grabbed Jones' arm and explained, "You think you're going to skip town, jump the next bus? You owe us two dimes, Ticks. We want it."

Jones pulled his arm free and winced. "Two dimes? I don't think that's much of a problem, gentlemen." His hand went back to his pocket and came out with a quarter. "Keep the change."

Not Hardly knocked it from his hand and snarled, "You think that's funny? You owe two grand!"

The coin hit the floor twenty feet away.

Now it was clear to Jones. Phil made a bad bet

on the Dodgers or the ponies. No wonder Phil wanted Jones to cover his shift—there was no parole officer…only thugs. It didn't pay to be Phil.

Mr. Tee took hold of the yellow sleeve again and squeezed. "What do you say we take a little walk and find that money somewhere."

"You got a piggy bank at home?" Not Hardly grinned and his partner laughed.

As Jones began his forced walk, they were startled by the sound of two hands clapping. Jones and his companions turned as one to notice a woman approaching them. "Very good! When I left the police station this morning…" she reached in her overcoat and flashed a badge, "I didn't know the bus station was doing theater. Phil, your talent is wasted on shoes, how can Broadway do without you? You other two I recognize. I've seen your rap sheets—I mean your resumes."

The three of them stared at her in silence.

"It has to be a one-act play, right? You wouldn't really be harassing my client, would you?"

Mr. Tee let go of Jones' arm.

She continued, "This might be a good time for the two of you to bow and exit…stage left."

That's what they did. They quickly bowed and

hurried for the door.

"Good riddance," she said. "Don't you think?"

Jones nodded. He caught a glimpse of himself escaping in his Lincoln Continental. A longshot, like a scene in a dream. What a morning.

"I'm that parole officer you've been expecting." She stuck out her hand, "Gracie Goodwin."

Jones shook her hand, "I'm Phil." Was it finally safe to say that?

"First of all, I'm glad you're employed, I'll make a note of that in my report. But I'd hate to include anything about gambling or getting into trouble with said activity. I promise, if I see you dabbling in *show biz* again, it won't end well. There won't be a standing ovation."

"I understand," Jones said, raising his sore arm. "Scout's honor. That was my last performance."

"Stick to shoes, Mr. Ticks. I don't want to run you in. By the way—how's business?"

"Fine." As soon as she was gone and the coast was clear, Jones decided he was done with shoe shining. He would lock up the grip and get on his bike and visit the real Phil Ticks. Phil had a lot of explaining to do.

Officer Goodwin had some paperwork for

Jones to sign, which he did, with a fake autograph and then after one more warning, she bid him goodbye. Her shoes clicked. He watched her stoop to pick up his quarter on her way.

Jones was glad to see her go. Phil better watch his step. After a minute observing the door in case she returned, Jones figured he was safe. He got the grip off the chair and ditched it in the locker. Another bus was loading in five minutes. They came and went all day and night. But he was done with them. He was sticking to bicycle riding.

Before he reached it, he slowed at the vending machine. It was about time for that coffee.

He looked at the price for a cup of instant. All he had to do was drop in some coins and press a black button and a paper cup would drop below the spigot and out would flow coffee. Miraculous. He counted his change. His finger hovered over his palm. "Just my luck," he said. He was a quarter shy.

UNDERWORLD INFINITY

The apartment was on the corner of Holly Street, across from the bank. Jones made it there in good time and went around back and took the rickety metal stairway up. He wanted some answers. There was no breeze. His bike waited for him on the ground. His noble steed. So much depends upon a red bicycle smudged with sunlight beside the rusted fire escape.

Phil Ticks looked outside, through an inch gap in the chained door.

"It's me," Jones said. "You set me up."

"I'm sorry, Jones. I hope you're okay. I'm heartbroken about it, but I got myself in deep. I panicked."

"What did you do to—"

"I owe them two dimes!"

"How did that happen?"

"It's called gambling, Jones. Sometimes you don't win. I got a shadow on me right now, but I'll get out. I won some today."

"What? While I was covering you at the bus station, you were—"

"I was at the dog track." He shrugged. "Guilty."

Jones groaned.

"I had to! How else am I going to come up with that kind of dough?"

"Who else is looking for you?"

"What do you mean who else?"

"When I got to your stand this morning, a couple of thugs grabbed me and knocked me out and threw me on a bus. I'd be dumped in Pasadena if I wasn't discovered. Hold on—" Jones paused, as a flash of Avalon appeared. "I *did* go somewhere." He tried to remember the dream of it.

"Uh oh," said Phil.

"It was beautiful."

"Oh no."

"Someone said you have a box?"

Phil winced. "Debt collectors I can deal with.

That comes with the territory. But those other guys aren't from around here. They're not even from this planet."

Jones scoffed. "Right."

"It's true! They're from Avalon."

The word startled Jones like an electric jolt. He saw a field full of yellow flowers, a car and a girl.

Phil knew that look, "You been there, haven't you, Jones? They sent you there, didn't they?"

"I don't know. I guess so. Is Avalon a dream?"

"You got that right, J! And brother, do I have something they want."

"Well, what is it?"

"I got plans. I got something big in the works. Something that'll get me back my two dimes and then some." An endless underworld of wheeling and dealing with no end in sight.

Jones drummed his fingers on the door and rolled his eyes. "Am I coming in or what?"

"You sure nobody followed?"

Jones looked behind himself, off the fire escape. Cars parked at the sidewalks and the bank parking lot. It reminded him he should get back to his own parking lot. If Phil would hurry up and spill the beans. "Nobody followed me."

Phil speedily took the latches off the door, four chains rattling as he drew the door open enough for Jones. "Hurry up!" Phil slammed the door after him and scratched the chains back into their tracks.

Phil's apartment was dim. The venetian blinds made thin stripes below the window. Drifting motes. There wasn't much to the room. Phil had pawned everything but a cot mattress on the floor.

Jones' tennis shoes echoed over to the window. He lifted a blind.

"Careful!"

Jones let go of the blind. "Tell me more about Avalon." He leaned against the wall. There were no chairs.

"It's not exactly a dream. I think it's a whole other world. There must be other worlds like ours, worlds where they did it different. Did you get to look around?"

Jones agreed. "You should have seen my trailer."

"Everything's better in Avalon. It's like Heaven, right? And who wouldn't want that? Once they get a taste, people will do anything to go back." He grinned, "That's why I thought, they'll pay top dollar to be there." He made a lightbulb going on in the air, then he pointed. "Wait a second, I'll be right back."

Jones waited. There were nail holes in the wall where picture frames used to be. Faint ghostly squares where the sun left their shadows. He heard cupboards opening and closing in the kitchen.

SELLING AVALON

Phil returned with a brown grip. It looked like the one Jones dumped in the station locker. "I can make the two grand, easy. Guess what I got in here."

Jones said, "More shoeshine gear?"

"No—never mind—you'd never guess." Phil kneeled and set the grip on the floor. "Get ready…" he opened the bag and reached both hands in to take out a box. "Says here on the label, Property of Avalon. And wait til you see what's inside…" He ran his hand over the top until it decided to open.

Jones was standing a few feet away, he wasn't sure it wasn't dangerous, but after it opened and the world didn't disappear, he came over close. "What are those?"

"This is how people go back and forth to Avalon." Little capsules. "They eat this stuff or—" he removed a syringe, "they shoot this into a vein and you're gone, brother."

"That's what they got my arm with," Jones said. "Is this why they're looking for you?"

"What do you think, JJ? Someone snitched on me. Avalon's after me. This stuff is dynamite."

Jones was about to say something.

"Hold on! I'm desperate, I finally hit it big. This unlocks Avalon, there's a market for this, I got a chance to get out of hock, JJ!" He shut the box and zippered it in the bag. "I just have to sell it before they get to me."

"Well, I'd say they're getting close."

Phil ignored that. He grabbed his coat and was putting it on when it occurred to him, "You know what?" He grinned and laughed, "Now they think you're me! They forgot what I look like. How crazy is that? That could buy me some time."

"Good for you, Phil, but what about me? Am I Public Enemy Number 1 in Avalon? Do I need to stay locked in my trailer hiding until this mess of yours blows over?"

Phil was unlocking the chains on the door. He turned, "It wouldn't hurt."

"Hang on a minute. Do you have a disguise or something? I have to get home somehow. I need a different suit or something." He groaned, "You know, my intuition told me not to answer the phone this morning, but did I listen? Thanks to you, I have maniacs from Avalon after me!"

Phil hushed him and nodded at the hallway behind the door. The hall could be full as a subway car with those Avalon maniacs. He left the door still attached by a chain and two deadbolts. "I'll take a look in my room and see what I got. I guess I owe you that."

Jones waited. On the wall by the door, there were more nail holes where picture frames used to be. Phil must have had a museum in here, before he fell on hard times and pawned everything and the museum became an empty tomb. Jones heard noise in the other room then footsteps.

Phil returned. "You get two choices..." He pulled a gorilla suit out of a paper grocery bag.

"What? No, it's not Halloween. I'd be hard to miss in that. I need a disguise. I need to melt in with the crowd."

Phil reached into the bag again, "Or I have these glasses."

"That's it?"

Phil shrugged and started to put them back in the grocery bag.

"Fine, I'll take the glasses. But what about another jacket or something? This yellow suit is my calling card. You got a raincoat?"

Phil took a moment to think, then he turned and carried his paper bag and grip to that other room of his. A closet door creaked.

Jones looked at his disguise. You could fool people in movies by putting on glasses. Maybe something that simple would work on those thugs from Avalon, maybe they would think he was Clark Kent or Cary Grant in a screwball comedy. When he tried them on, he didn't see much of a change.

Phil's voice carried from the other room, "I think I found something..." Footsteps. He reappeared with a Mexican poncho. "I got this in Juarez."

What could Jones do? It was either that or a gorilla suit. If there was a mirror that wasn't pawned, it might have dissuaded Jones, but he had no choice. He put the poncho on and said, "Fine," he was ready for the world outside.

Before the last bolt unlocked, Phil stopped and wagged the leather grip, "Oh, by the way…Do you want some of this Avalon?"

Jones' glass eyes blinked.

"Before I sell it off. Once it's gone, it's gone. You've been there, you know the feeling. And who knows if you'll get the chance to go back. Since you're my friend, I'll give you two for one."

His beady eyes shone like the devil himself. Jones knew Phil wouldn't have any trouble selling off Avalon.

CONFESSIONS OF A PAWN SHOP

They went their separate ways at the street, Phil towards downtown and Jones pushing his bike up the hill. Jones watched Phil hurry across Holly. Jones was in a different hurry, all this Avalon business had him worried. He kept his arms under his poncho draped over the handlebars. When Jones caught his reflection in a shop window, he stopped. His new disguise needed some toning down. A little cohesion would be good. A sombrero would work. Behind his reflection was a pawnshop. He supposed Phil had a running tab going there. Strange that Phil sold everything else he had, but he held on to a gorilla suit and a lurid poncho. He could have got a few dollars for them anyway.

Jones was no stranger to pawn shops. That's

where he bought his bike, after his car died. If there was a way he could have driven a ghost Lincoln Continental, he would have—wouldn't that put the criminal world on edge, to hear the growl of a 200 horsepower V8 engine and the appearance of a man driving in a cloud—but the best Jones could do on his budget was a ten-dollar bike at Rerun's Second Chance. He made up a story about a birthday girl and managed to talk the owner down to eight bucks.

Right away, Jones spotted what he wanted. It could have been spotlit, with violins and guitars. He had first seen one on a black and white TV, with horses stomping the desert sand and cowboys whooping. When he was eight, he wanted to be a hero wearing that. It was a Tom Mix ten-gallon hat. The perfect accessory for a gaucho's poncho.

The hat had its own shelf. It demanded it. It was a crown in a museum. It had history.

Why did the cowboy hock his hat? It sounded like the start of a joke. It was no joke though. Everything in here had a story, mostly sad. Was it plucked from a dying gunman in a skid row flophouse? Well, whatever the explanation, Jones decided it belonged to him now.

Wrapping his hands around the felt, Jones picked it up and settled it on his head. It had the weight of an eagle and the brim stuck out like wings. "I love it," he said. He shuffled over to a mirror and his eight-year-old self agreed. The hat even made him a foot and a half taller.

He swaggered to the counter. With the hat on, Jones Jr. was practically gone, except for the yellow suit pants and white tennis shoes. "How do I look?" he asked the woman behind the counter. "Not bad, huh?"

"I guess," she said. One hand sat near an ashtray. She tapped the cigarette. Then when she told him the price, the conversation stopped.

Jones didn't have much, his pocket change wasn't enough for a cup of coffee, but he had an inspired idea. "I'd like you to put this on Phil Ticks' tab."

"Is that you?"

"Of course it's me. I do a steady business here. I'm sure I have credit coming to me."

She put a notebook on the counter and leafed through the pages to the Ts.

It worked. It might have been the first time that being Phil Ticks worked.

APPOINTMENT WITH A MUMMY

The spirit of Tom Mix rode with Jones. While he pedaled his bike on the road out of town, what a pleasant mile of sunshine it was, spun along like a horse on wheels beside the sea.

The parking lot was pretty full of cars. On the weekend you needed a shoehorn to clear them. As Jones drifted through the gateposts, he was thinking of Avalon, the little house with the porch that was supposed to be where the trailer was. So much for Avalon.

The big Stetson acted as a sort of parachute slowing his glide into the lot. He arced around a family carrying buckets and blankets and parasols. A day at the beach. He could hear the ocean and the sounds people made in response to sun, water and the tidal pull of the moon.

When he was in Avalon, he had a sign. He remembered it: Jones Jr. Detective. If he couldn't have a house, at least he could have that sign. There were paint cans under the sink. All he needed was a board to hang on the front door. What happens if you conjure something from Avalon, will that beautiful world follow?

On top of the trailer, a seagull watched him roll up. It was the same gull from the morning. For some reason it had taken a liking to Jones, or maybe it was still waiting for toast. An animal gets used to a routine. If he kept it up, Jones would have a friend. The bird could help him if Jones got lost in the fog at sea and couldn't find land. Being kind to animals can have all sorts of benefits. All Jones thought he was doing was tossing out crust, he didn't know there was trust. A seagull on your side can see more than a camera.

Jones dismounted in the Schwinn's usual spot. There's no way he could have predicted the places the morning took him. Jones rubbed his sore arm and thought of Tom Mix and all that cowboy's wounds: gunshots, fractures, circus accidents, stunts gone wrong. Sure, Mix had trouble in the Old West and Hollywood, but he never tangled with Avalon.

The sorry, rusted trailer was a sight for sore eyes. Its vision shined on the lenses of his glasses. The day's *Herald* was rolled on the cement doorstep slab. The paper and a pot of coffee bubbling on the stove would go a long way to making things better. With a wheeze, Jones bent and reached out of his poncho to get the newspaper, then he opened the door. It wasn't locked. It didn't need to be.

"Halt, who goes there?" said the robot standing behind the door.

"It's me, Roscoe. I'm incognito."

The tall metal robot shuffled aside. "You surprised me."

"This is nothing. You're lucky I'm not wearing the gorilla costume."

Roscoe buzzed and clicked. He didn't know what that sentence meant.

Jones rounded his friend and tossed the *Herald* on the table, along with his cowboy hat. He took off his poncho and his suitcoat and left them on the chair. "Did you hear anything interesting on the radio?"

The robot shut the door and approached. Each footstep sounded like a big toolbox picked up and dropped. "Not much happening so far. A 10-91 stuck in a tree. A 415 at Thrifty and another one at a carwash. A 411 at Grant Street. A mummy walked out of the museum and caught a cab. A—"

"Woah!"

"There's more."

"No, I like the mummy one."

Roscoe paused, "Do you know how many mummies there are in this town?"

"Not many?"

"Exactly. It would be like finding a needle in a haystack. Are you prepared to chase down clues on something that barely exists?"

"Well…let me know if you hear anything suspicious. I wouldn't mind a nice mummy caper. But first…" Jones finished pouring water in a pan and set it on the stove. "I was thinking I'd like to sit down with a cup of coffee and read the paper. After that, I'd like to paint a sign for the door."

"A For Rent sign? Are we finally moving somewhere that doesn't make me rust?"

"No."

"What kind of sign?"
"It's something I saw in Avalon."

THE CLEOPATRA DRIFT

There it was on the door, a white painted board with black letters across it spelling out: **Jones Jr. Detective**. He took a few steps back from the sign and gave it a good look. Why did it take him so long to do this? Like a dream, Avalon prompted him and he obeyed. There was a better world in this spot that he was doing his best to recreate. "I don't know," he said to himself, "This looks pretty good."

"What's a junior detective?"

Jones gave a little jump of surprise. He turned around.

A lady fresh from the beach, on her way back to her car. She continued, "Sounds like you're ten.

Either that or you only investigate people named Jones Jr. which couldn't be very lucrative for you."

There's always a critic ready to pounce on something beautiful.

Did he need to explain? Who was she?

"But if your *name* is Jones Jr., I think you could use a comma before the word detective. Or a separate line perhaps."

"Thanks," he said. "But I ran out of paint. This is the finished product."

She pursed her lips. "Really? Not even enough paint for a comma?"

He turned his palms up, empty, dramatically.

"I can bring you some tomorrow."

"That's okay. Honestly, it's meant to be the way it is. I saw it in a dream."

"Ohhh," she nodded. "Dreams have their own rules."

But he could tell it still bothered her. "Tell you what though…if you find a comma somewhere, on a tree branch or on the sidewalk, wherever it might be, bring it by. We can see if it wants to be on the sign."

She smiled. Her dark eyes sparkled. "I'll do that." She was holding a book in one hand—no wonder, it was probably full of commas, Jones thought—and she tucked it into a bag so she could offer a free hand. "I'm Zahra."

"Nice to meet you. I'm Jones." Her hand was soft and cool as new soap.

"I've seen you before," said Zahra. "I've been wanting to say hello. I don't know what I was waiting for."

"You were waiting for punctuation."

Zahra laughed. "You *are* a detective."

Against the blue sky, the same old seagull on the roof of the trailer watched them talk. It looked like a chimney, quiet, still waiting for toast. The picture of that crust was foremost in its mind. The world was just a backdrop to that starring attraction.

While the seagull's favorite movie was playing, Jones and Zahra said goodbye until next time.

Jones watched her cross the parking lot, then looked at the roof, at the sound of the gull. They were always crying. When he looked for Zahra again, she was already in her car. Over the tops of cars, he heard an engine start. She was from Egypt. That was interesting. Where Cleopatra drifted through time.

He turned and took a couple steps closer to his

trailer. The sign looked fine, but maybe a comma wouldn't hurt. Why not? He pictured Zahra with a butterfly net being very careful in a vacant lot as she approached a comma that was resting on a spar of rebar. She would bring it to him tomorrow in a clear jam jar.

X-RAY SPECTACLES

Someone knocked on the door. It was going on evening. One thing Roscoe couldn't do was fumble the door open. If only Jones Sr. had given him hands instead of thick grasping claws. Over the years Sr. made lots of improvements to Roscoe like giving him the power of speech and the ability to creel police dispatches from the air. Sr. had a goal in mind. Roscoe was going to be a companion and stalwart defender of his son, but time took over as it does with all things. Towards the end, all the old man could do was sit in his chair by the window and watch. No more wizardry. His son had no aptitude for inventions, Jr. wanted to be a detective and solve mysteries that baffled everyone else. Helping as best he could, Roscoe stood by the door like a butler. "Who goes there?" he buzzed.

"Is Jones there?"

A woman's voice. Perhaps. One time Jones Sr. showed Roscoe a cardboard box labeled Roscoe II. It contained blueprints, parts and tangled bits of circuitry for the modifications he wanted to do. With shaking spotted hands mottled by age, Sr. turned the flaps on top and he found a comic book, folded to a page of advertisements. Jones Sr. tapped a yellow fingernail on a picture in the corner. **X-Ray Spectacles Only $1. Scientific, optical principle really works.** A drawing of a kid wearing them, staring at a woman's silhouette. If only Roscoe had been adapted to wear those, he could have seen through the door and known for sure if a woman was waiting. "One moment, please," the sturdy robot replied.

"What is it, Roscoe?" Jones lay on the bed folded down from the tin wall. His question came through the cone of the ten-gallon hat placed over his face.

"Are you still sleeping?"

"I'm not sleeping, Roscoe, I'm thinking. I have

so much on my mind today."

"There's a visitor at the door."

Jones had been sleeping of course. He groaned with the effort of sitting up, settling the hat atop the blankets before he swung his legs to the floor. "Tell them I'm on the way." He had about twenty feet to cover.

Roscoe told the door, "He's on the way."

"Thank you."

Jones was wearing slippers when he got there. "Thanks, Roscoe," he mumbled. He briefly wondered, when was the last time Roscoe left the trailer? Could he even fit out the door? Funny it never occurred to Jones before—the robot was like a story he heard. A friend of a friend made a boat inside his house during the winter. Every cold day he cut and planed cedar ribs and planking. He wanted to be one of the first boaters on the lake that April. The poor guy had to tear down a wall to get his boat there.

The door swerved open and there she was—the girl from Avalon.

"Hello," said Frida.

Jones was speechless. Imagine someone you've seen in a dream just a few hours before coming to your door.

She said, "Can I come in? Can we talk inside?"

"Yes," he managed to say.

She walked past him and the robot didn't bother her as she stopped in the middle of the trailer and looked around herself. "It's a little different than Avalon," she said.

"You're really here?" Jones felt dumb for saying it—of course she was here—you didn't need a detective to notice that. "I mean, why are you here? How?"

She sat on a chair by the table. A cereal bowl, a nearly empty coffee cup. "We have a problem, Jones. Avalon needs to hire you to find your friend Phil Ticks."

Jones took a wild guess, *It's about the box, right?* But he didn't say it aloud. Despite all the trouble Phil caused, Jones had known him too long to hand him over to Avalon. Although...it might be an improvement for Phil...No poverty, no debt collectors. Then again, Jones doubted if there were horse tracks there.

"Jones, I'm not here for long, do you know where he is?"

It was extraordinary, he was hypnotized by the

sight of her. This couldn't be happening...Unless he was still sleeping. Was he always sleeping, was everything a dream?

Frida rolled her eyes and came close and gently shook his shoulders.

That was even worse, he could smell Avalon on her, those fields and flowers and salt of the sea, the soft upholstery of a Lincoln Continental.

"For goodness sake, Jones."

"You're an angel," he blurted and immediately realized he said it. He wished the shadow of that ten-gallon hat was covering him, a grown man stammering like a mockingbird.

Frida had two more minutes before she would vanish. She had to make it clear to Jones. She showed him a capsule in her hand. "We take one of these and we can leave Avalon to come here. We cross over to—well, *why* we do doesn't matter—Avalon has a responsibility to care for your world. But someone stole a box full of these. We have reason to believe your friend Phil Ticks has it. That's how you got drawn into this, Jones. We're desperate to get it back. America's not ready for Avalon."

Jones was still a little lost in the closeness of

her.

"Here," she gave him a capsule. "If you can get the box, please take this medicine and bring our box to Avalon. Does that make sense?"

"Yes."

"Please find it," she repeated. She closed his hand around the capsule. "Oh—money—what's your detective rate?"

That was automatic with him, it was something he told anyone who asked, the words came from him like a warbly tape recording, "$200 a day, plus expenses."

Frida put a roll of bills in his other hand. She smiled. Then she was gone.

She didn't feel any more real than a dream and when she disappeared, Jones' hands were empty.

6 PM ON CHANNEL 12

Suspended from the hanger on the wall was a black raincoat. Jones got that and a pair of plaid pants one of his old clients, a clown, gave him. When the circus lost an elephant, they hired Jones and he found the beast eventually, at the edge of a tarpit that Jones got stuck in. That was the end of his first yellow seersucker suit.

Roscoe said, "While you were sleeping, there was—"

"I wasn't sleeping, I was meditating."

The robot continued, "I heard an update on that mummy."

It took Jones a moment to remember the mummy that escaped from the museum. That mystery was a detective's dream! But could he solve two mysteries at once? Could he find the missing Avalon *and* a mummy? "What was it?"

"There was a 10-70 at the Thrifty grocery."

"You know I don't know all those codes, Roscoe. They're easy for *you* to memorize, they're stamped in your memory banks."

"10-70 is a shoplifting incident. The manager said it was a mummy."

Jones put on his big hat. "That's great." He got his glasses off the shelf. "That's just great. I'm hooked! Reel me in, Thrifty. Who knows—if I'm lucky maybe I'll see Phil there and tie it all up in a mummy bow."

"If Frida comes back, should I tell her you're on the job?"

"Yeah, you better. And ask her about my fee. That Avalon money doesn't work here."

"And if your other new ingenue wants to speak with you?"

"Zahra?"

"I believe that was her name, yes."

"Roscoe—I don't know what you're implying, I'm not Cyrano de Bergerac. Tell her the truth. Tell her I'm investigating a mummy and a stolen box of Avalon."

"Okay, as you wish."

"Not to mention I have Phil's loan sharks after me." Jones zippered his raincoat. "I don't think they believe I'm not him." The poncho disguise was too warm. His old yellow suit rocked on the hanger. Much as he wanted to, he couldn't wear it again until the coast was clear. Mumbling, he sat and tied his sneaker laces and stood up.

Roscoe had a last question. "Before you go, could you do me a favor? Could you turn on the TV? *Barney Miller* is on." He clacked his claws helplessly.

"There. Let me know if you hear anything else about the mummy. I'll have my walkie-talkie." The TV screen was filled with a moody black and white snowstorm. "I don't know how you can watch that thing, I can't see a thing." Voices murmured from it, full of static.

Roscoe laughed. He was controlling transmission. If he wished to make it louder, he would bring up the volume. If he wished to make it softer, he would tune it to a whisper. He controlled the horizontal, he controlled the vertical. He could roll the image, make it flutter. He could change the focus to a soft blur or sharpen it to crystal clarity. There was nothing wrong with their television set.

"What's so funny?" It looked like cotton rain to Jones and sounded just the same.

"Fish said something."

"My dad liked that show, didn't he?"

It was true. Every Thursday night at 9 the robot and Jones Sr. would watch *Barney Miller*. That was their version of tossing the ball in the backyard. Roscoe caught the show on reruns now, at 6 PM on Channel 12. He remembered every show, but something was missing: Jones Sr.

Jones opened the trailer door. The low sun painted shadows. He didn't feel like riding his bike to town again. Pedaling back on the road in the dark in time to chain the entrance. Besides, how long would that mummy linger near the grocery? "Hey Roscoe. Why don't you call me a cab. I'll sit out here and wait for it."

"Okay," the robot replied. "When the commercial comes on."

Jones went around the tin corner where his bicycle was parked. He grabbed his walkie-talkie and reached for an aluminum chair. With a little effort the aluminum unfolded. His clown pants settled creaking into the uneasy chair. There were still some cars in the lot, not as many, they were starting to wander home. A devoted audience would stay until the sun popped out of sight into the Pacific.

Now that Jones was outside, Roscoe finetuned the TV frequency. That was one of the updates that came from the Roscoe II cardboard box. Who knows where the old man was leading him with all those adjustments and innovations. Barney Miller's station room was real as 1978 used to be and clear as a bell. A satellite could hear the ring, pick it up and throw a bouncing signal at the moon, and Mars and Venus, and ricochet it out beyond our solar system where human life was waiting to be known.

THE PARAFFIN TEST

The taxi dropped him off at Thrifty. In the night, people fluttered in and out of the glowing grocery like moths. Jones put his wallet back into his raincoat. He had a couple fives and some ones. He felt rich. And hungry. When the doors slid open, he saw food everywhere. Tempting as it was, the job came first. Job? Nobody had hired him, not yet. But when he showed up at the museum with their mummy in tow, he was sure there'd be a reward. 3,000 years ago when they sealed a mummy in a sarcophagus, it was meant to stay put.

Thrifty looked like it returned to normal. Shoppers pushing carts. Jones didn't see any police.

That was fine by Jones, he did better without them around. He liked running his own show. He just needed some answers. "Excuse me," he said.

A store clerk holding soup cans turned around.

"Can I ask you something?"

"Sure."

"Can you tell me about the mummy?" Jones fished out his wallet and showed his private investigator's license.

The clerk set the cans down, "The cops were already here."

"I know. But sometimes they miss things. Did you see it?"

"Yeah, I was shelving, same as I'm doing now, and I saw the mummy. We get a lot of oddballs in here." His eyes darted up at Jones' ten-gallon hat. "I try not to judge. As long as they pay, but that mummy was stealing. He stuffed a can into his wrappers. I told him 'Hey!' and he took off."

"What did he steal? Do you know?"

The clerk nodded, "I'll show you." He took Jones down the aisle, reached up and pointed at a gap between other cans. "He stole tana leaves. It was the only can. We've had it on this shelf for ages, nobody wanted it. Look—you can see where he touched the shelf. Hey," he brightened, "maybe you can dust for fingerprints!"

"We're not going to find any prints. Not if it was a mummy. They're prepackaged."

"It was a mummy alright." The store manager appeared like a paratrooper dropped into Aisle 4 behind them. "And we already have a detective on the scene, mister. Jeff, you can get back to work."

"Yes, Mr. Schultz."

Jones said, "There's another detective here?"

"Yes. In baked goods. He's doing a paraffin test for prints. He showed up with the police. I don't know why they aren't searching outside though. That mummy couldn't go a mile on the back of a pickup truck. It can't have gone far."

"Where's baked goods?" Jones asked.

"End of the aisle, turn left."

"Thanks. And thanks for your help, Jeff." Jones tipped his huge hat. Jones' robot Roscoe wasn't the only one with access to a police scanner, a lot of private investigators used them to get a jump on the competition. The phonebook was full of detectives trying to make a living. The end of Aisle 4 had a red and white pyramid of stacked canned evaporated milk.

"Oh no..." Jones groaned. The other detective was no stranger, it was Kent Washington, busily applying paraffin wax to a large box of donuts. Even worse than his being there was his appearance there. Kent was wearing a yellow seersucker suit just like Jones's.

As Jones got closer, he heard Washington tell a baker behind the counter, "I'll have to take this box to the lab. We'll give it a full analysis."

The baker shrugged, he was busy, he had to take four sheet cakes out of the oven.

Jones said, "You still pulling that paraffin gag?"

Kent pressed his finger to his lips. "C'mon Jones. Keep it down." There were twenty donuts in the box.

Jones pinched a fold of the yellow suit, "What's with the wardrobe? For some reason it looks familiar to me."

"What's with yours?" Washington countered.

"I asked you first."

"You should be flattered, Jones. I'm a fan, okay? You've got a reputation. Or your suit does."

"You thought you could get the job if you looked like me?"

"No hard feelings, Jones. We do what we can."

Washington put the wax away in his kit bag, picked up the bakery box and winked, "Even if I can't solve it, at least I got some donuts." He was proud of himself. "Later, Jones." What an exit! Out the doors, he scratched under the slick box lid and freed a pastry. He was king of detectives, all the way until the middle of the parking lot when two thugs spotted the yellow suit and closed in.

Meanwhile, Jones got directions out the back of Thrifty. He wanted to check the loading dock, the shadows around the dumpsters. It would be quiet and dark, a safe place for the mummy to catch its breath. If it needed breath.

A hall with a buzzing flickering light led to the exit. A note was taped to the door: **Did you remember to clock out?** signed Schultz. Jones was no stranger to jobs like this, up at 6 AM, a manager breathing down your neck, "get back to work," stress and worry—ugh, he counted himself lucky to be self-employed.

An algae green light bathed the cement dock. This was where the clerks and cashiers would come for a break. There was evidence, crushed out cigarettes, an empty bottle by a chair leg, a paperback with warped pages. A black night sky. A few bright stars. Jones went to the crumbled edge where delivery trucks had rubbed and bumped the concrete. There was just enough room on the tar below for trucks to pull in and turn around. It was dark beyond. A murky chain-link fence too tall for a mummy to vault. Jones took a narrow set of steps down.

He noticed something.

Caught on the fence, it writhed in the breeze. A ghostly strand moving like an underwater weed. A pale sliver of cloth. He didn't need a paraffin test to know who it belonged to.

TEN-GALLON HEIST

"Is this a new look?"

"I'm trying it out," Jones said.

"Let me guess..." she said. "You're investigating a crime at a kid's birthday party? No, that's not it—you've given up on being a detective, you're one of those rodeo clowns. You hide in a barrel while a bull knocks you around."

"I'm still in the same trade, Linda. As a matter of fact, I have two clients right now."

"Well, I hope they have better luck than me."

He winced. It was years ago, but his first case still haunted him. He really blew it. If only he could do things differently. If only they could both forget.

She said, "Do you know what you want?"
"Yes."
"Surprise me."
"I'll have the chili please. And a coffee."

She didn't need to write it down. It was always the same with him.

When she left, he removed his cowboy hat, flipped it upside down and set it across from him. It took up most of the tabletop. He couldn't make up for the past, but he tried. He came to this café often as he could and ordered what he could afford. If he could get that Avalon money to work, he'd come back and leave her a big tip.

The night was warm. Cars drove past, people on the busy sidewalk passed his table and gave him a glance. Jones stared at the candle flickering in a jar by his hat and walkie-talkie. He had to keep his thoughts on the present, he had come a long way. He was a better detective now, admired even. Look at Kent Washington—he wanted to *be* Jones Jr. A different waitress brought him a bowl and a cup. A moonflower tree grew overhead. The blossoms competed with the stale air of the road, murmuring of better things than engines. It was a lot of work for one tree.

He ate his chili, sipped at his coffee, accepted a refill when it was nearly done. The waitress was friendly, she must have been new. It was almost time to head back to the trailer. He had to lock up the parking lot or it would drift away. The Pacific would pull it like a carpet. Imagine it washing up on some tropical shore in an Indonesian archipelago. That was probably every parking lot's dream.

The waitress left his bill, smiled, "When you're ready, no rush."

Jones fished out his wallet and realized while he had enough to pay, how was he going to catch a taxi home? He certainly couldn't ask Linda for the fare, not after their history. This was his penance, coming here for chili was his slow way of making it up to her. The moonflower was sowing fragrance, the candlelight shook, a detective's mind must always be nimble enough to jump.

He got a pen from his pocket and wrote: **Need Taxi Money** on the napkin. Also: **Please**. Underlined. He draped the desperate message over the rim of his hat, held down by a quarter, facing the street. Cupping his coffee, he put on the face of someone under the heel of the world, and by some miracle, perhaps magic, perhaps pity, it didn't take long for the first coin to be tossed his way, and then another, and another. When it rains, it pours.

The waitress made her round outside with the pot of coffee. She didn't know the nature of the Tom Mix hat, she couldn't read the napkin from her vantage point. "Would you like another refill?"

"Oh sure," Jones pushed the cup towards her. "Maybe one more for the road." It was about time to go. "Do you know what time it is?"

She finished pouring and looked at her slim wristwatch and told him.

Jones sat up straight, electrified, "Really?! I gotta go!" He emptied his wallet on the table and grabbed his hat, heaved it up to his head and plopped it down, spilling a waterfall of quarters, dimes, nickels and pennies all over.

SUBMARINE TELEPHONE BOOTH

A robot claw shaking him woke Jones. The trailer was fuzzy with blue morning light. "Wuzzut?" Jones croaked.

"I just intercepted a 10-63."

Jones rubbed his eyes and whined, "I told you, Roscoe, I don't know those codes."

"An attempted kidnapping at the museum. Victim described his assailant as a mummy."

"He's on the move!" Jones quickly stood. "Could you start some coffee for me? I gotta get going." He looked at the clock and made a face. He hadn't slept long enough to dream. The birds were just starting to sing. While Jones aimed for the narrow bathroom door, Roscoe shuffled over to the stove.

Last night, Jones had enough in change to make it home with 47 cents left over. He kept eleven dollars in a coffee can in the cupboard. That was the emergency mad-money fund. It would cover a cab to the museum. When he went to the table for his coffee, he was wearing his plaid clown pants, a maroon sweater, and a tan fedora. He was carrying his raincoat.

Roscoe stood at the little porthole shining like a submarine.

"Thanks for the coffee. Wait until you see this, Roscoe." Jones sat and put his coat on top of the table. "Look." He retrieved the mummy cloth. "I found this on the fence at Thrifty. What do you think?" Jones took a sip of coffee. It was hot but not too hot. He expected Roscoe to date the scrap to the Third Dynasty.

"Is it part of a kite?"

"What? A kite? Are you kidding me? It's a piece off that mummy!"

"I'm afraid you're mistaken." Lights flashed in the robot's eyes. "This is a synthetic fiber."

An old vaudeville standby was the spit-take.

It wasn't pretty, but it was a guaranteed laugh for Abbott and Costello.

Not so funny for a robot though. Spills and accidents meant work. Roscoe got a towel to clean the coffee. A robot's work is never finished.

"What do you mean, Roscoe?"

"I deduce a child was flying it. From the wear and fading of the material I'd guess this happened last summer."

"A kite, huh? That's impressive, Roscoe. You'd make quite a detective. Say, you're not trying to replace me, are you?"

The robot claw returned the cloth. "Elementary deduction." Thanks to Jones Sr. and his Roscoe II carton for installing a Sherlock 4000 circuit.

"Well, anyway..." Jones paused for more coffee, the cup was nearly empty, "This much we know..." another dramatic pause to napkin his mouth, "In the space of a day and night, a mummy snuck out of the museum, went on a shoplifting spree, and returned to the museum. Let me offer a little elementary deduction of my own: I think he's still there. What do you think of that, Roscoe?"

"I came to a similar conclusion."

"There!" Jones tapped his temple, "See! What's

that saying? Great minds think alike." He gulped the rest of his coffee.

"Great minds think alike, but fools seldom differ."

"What? No—that's not it. Just the first part, about great minds. I tell you what, Roscoe. When I get there, I'm going to search that museum and find that mummy." He stood up and put on his raincoat. When he reached the door, as he was reaching for the handle and the beach parking lot was only a few steps away, the robot stopped him with a question.

"Aren't you also supposed to be on the case for Miss Frida from Avalon?"

"When she pays me in real dollars, then I'll start looking for Phil Ticks." He opened the door and paused on the stair below with a sigh. "Ohhhh, alright. I guess it wouldn't hurt to call Phil…see if he's around…I still need to call for a taxi anyway."

Jones returned to the table and his empty cup and pulled the phone towards himself. "You remember Phil's number?" he asked.

Roscoe also served as telephone book and rolodex. He promptly answered.

The rotary dial responded, clicked and spun.

Jones drummed his fingers while he listened to a ring.

Phil wasn't at his apartment. Or if he was, he wasn't answering. The telephone must have been pealing like Notre Dame in that echo chamber room. Jones was about to hang up when a hoary voice barked in his ear, "Who is it?"

"Is Phil there?"

"No!"

"This is the number I have for his apartment."

"Well, unless he lives in a telephone booth, this ain't it!"

That was all. The background sound of a street somewhere fell silent as the connection was broken.

Jones said, "You sure that's Phil's number?"

Roscoe folded his arms.

"Yeah," Jones said, "I know. You know everything." He hung up the phone. "It's weird… That was the number for a telephone booth. I guess…I guess he doesn't have a phone. No wonder, he sold off everything but my glasses and a poncho. And that gorilla suit in a grocery bag, let's not forget that. A lot of good that will do him. Oh well…It's time to go." He picked up the receiver again. It hummed against his ear like a content honeybee. "What's the taxicab number?"

VIOLET ZEN

Jones pulled his bicycle out of the taxi trunk and rolled it onto the sidewalk. The cab rattled off into traffic as Jones steered his bike towards one of the big stone lions guarding the museum stairway. There was just enough room to push the Schwinn between the hedge and lock it to the lion's leg. If he thought that lion would protect his bike, he couldn't have been more wrong.

The museum wasn't open yet, but there were lights on inside, probably police in there too, probably a detective or two horning in on Jones' investigation. He left his bicycle and chuffed up the stairs.

A school bus across the street was waiting for

the museum to open. The bus was full of third graders. A girl in the window was watching Jones and as soon as he was out of sight, her imagination went to work on the red bicycle and the lion. The lion led the bicycle by the lock chain the way you would walk a dog. They were going to the park where they could push leaves into the pond and pretend they were boats, but on the way they would stop at the bakery to get banana bread, the same kind the girl liked to eat, with butter and some strawberry jam.

Instead of following the cement to the locked entrance doors, Jones went around the side, looking for another way in. He had to squeeze around another hedge. The museum was big as an ocean liner with all the windows gold with morning sun. He passed a dinosaur skeleton staring at him. The place was filled with history that would have stayed underground forever if it wasn't for people digging it up. Jones was no different, he was here to uncover a mystery. A caveman dummy held a club up to the glass.

When he reached the corner, Jones heard something. He peered around.

A janitor heaved a black bag into a dumpster.

He started work at 4 AM, he was tired, it was time for a break. He thumped the dumpster lid closed and went a little further away to a cement barricade he could sit on. That's where he rested and pawed under his blue overall and got a pack of cigarettes.

A detective relies on events like this, that seem to happen as if some pulp writer is helping the plot along. Jones hurried lightly on his sneaker soles for the open door. He looked over his shoulder quickly before he snuck in.

The janitor's back was haloed by a puff of smoke.

The door opened to a dull hallway with another door at the far end. Jones' shoes squeaked.

He opened that next door and met another detective on the other side.

Actually, she referred to herself as a sleuth. In the middle of a storage room filled with floor to ceiling shelves holding antiquities, Violet Zen was scribbling in her notebook. This would become another story for her column 'Where and When with Zen' that ran in the *Herald*.

"Hello Violet," Jones said.

She stopped writing and a smile appeared. "Jones Jr.! What took you so long? Oh, I remember—"

she tapped the pen on her notebook, "You ride a kid's bike, don't you?" She took great delight in that. She even ran a story about it in the newspaper. Complete with a grainy photograph of him wobbling along Holly Street. Two weeks before that bombshell, her column was devoted obituary-style to the demise of his Lincoln Continental. The photo for that column resembled a gangland killing, the car crunched up against the brick wall in a black splash of oil.

"Any more PIs here?" he asked.

"No," she replied. "Just us. And I think I have everything I need." She opened her notebook and read, "Let's see…police report, check…interview with officers on duty, check…interview with the victim, check…photographs, check…" She stopped flicking pages, "Say, would you mind if I get a picture of you, maybe with one of those Stone Age creatures out there? It would look great in my piece."

"I'm afraid I'm going to decline the offer, Violet. I'd like to conduct my own investigation right now. Which way to the victim? Who is it anyway?"

She ran a finger over her lips to indicate her lips

were sealed. Then she broke the seal. "You'll have to read my article, Jones. But out of professional courtesy, I believe you'll find his office through that door and to the right. Room 116."

"Thanks Violet. You're alright even if you're pretending not to be."

He opened the door out. It led to a broom closet. There was also a grimy mop in a yellow wheeled bucket.

"Oh, my mistake," Violet grinned. "I meant that other door, to your left."

Jones shook his head. Despite it all, he liked her. The detective guild was a family, she and Jones and Kent Washington and the rest of them. He expected to see a skeleton hanging in another closet when he tried the handle, but he opened the door to a hallway and he didn't look back.

Right and left were more doors. Fluorescent ceiling panels shined squares on the waxy floor. Zen told him 116. Knowing her it was another trick, but what did he have to lose? They were all rivals, but they weren't out to utterly sabotage each other. There was an element of support and respect among the detectives.

His shoes chirped to Room 116. A plaque

under the number read **CUSTODIAN**.

Jones called, "Very funny, Zen."

One of the doors in the long row down the hall opened and a stricken looking man stuck out his head. The relief of seeing Jones was palpable. "I heard footsteps. I thought you were the mummy coming back."

No thanks to Violet, Jones found what he was looking for.

WANTED:- An Egyptian Mummy. Will pay $5,000 for suitable specimen. Prof. Thaddeus Hicks, 154 Elm Road.

LEANDRO HIPHENOU

Leandro Hiphenou was gaunt, papery almost. He sat down at a desk crowded with photocopy stacks, stapled essays, journals, printouts. The walls of the office were lined with books, jammed together like bricks. A framed murky photo of Boris Karloff.

"You sure read a lot," Jones observed. If he lit a cigarette and dropped the match, the room would ignite instantly and take Hiphenou with its flash.

Leandro tightly clasped his hands and stared at the floor in silence. The mummy really shook him. He was an Egyptologist, you'd think the sight of a mummy would be old hat, but this one was alive. The icy cold hands had grabbed his arms and pulled him from the room. He was lucky to get away. He replayed the same story he told the police and Violet Zen, starting when he came to his office early to prepare for his lecture at the university.

That's when Jones mentioned all the books again. "I can't get over the library you've got. You must be an expert on mummies."

Leandro flustered, "Hardly. All I know about mummies is what I've seen in the movies. Otherwise, I just make the stuff up. It was so long ago, you can tell students anything. I tell them about marvelous things: escalators in the pyramids, solar power subways, airplanes that ran on honey and fluttered palm leaf wings. Copper submarines that used to go up the Nile."

"I don't think any of that's true, Mr. Hiphenou."

"I know, but they eat it up."

Jones angled to get their conversation on track, "Do you think this is the same mummy that escaped yesterday?"

"I'm sure of it."

"Why did it come back to the museum?"

Leandro said, "I brought it to life. I was foolish.

I was blind as George Zucco in *The Mummy's Ghost*. I'm fated to catastrophe, just like *The Mummy's Curse*. I know it will return."

"Why?"

"For divination. It wants me to prepare the tana leaves it stole, to make a brew so it can see through time to find her reincarnation."

"Wait—who?"

"The princess. The one he loved in Egypt all those thousands of years ago."

"Listen Mr. Hiphenou, I'm not one of those dewy-eyed students of yours. If you expect me to believe—"

"If you can accept a mummy on the loose, as surely you do, why else would you be here, you must accept where it's coming from and what it's capable of. When you stare into the bowl of brewed tana leaves, through the swirling mists of time, you will understand everything."

"And this is the story you told the cops?"

"No...not quite. I left out some of the details. Their perception only goes so far."

"And Miss Zen?"

"I told her what makes her readers buy papers. I'm scared, Mr. Jones. I know where this is going.

I need your help."

"I charge $200 a day, plus expenses."

"That seems reasonable." An alarm clock clattered and Leandro winced. He dug through the papers on his desktop, found the clock and switched the racket off. "I'm due at my lecture now. I haven't prepared, I don't know what I'll make up. Do you want to escort me to the class?"

"No. School's not for me. I had enough of that. Let me know when you're done, we can meet back here, I'd like to see what those tana leaves can do."

Hiphenou pointed at the tin can. "There they are. Waiting for boiling water. Would two o'clock work?"

"Sure."

"What a relief." Hiphenou gathered a handful of papers, some from this stack, some from over there, and Jones had to admit it made him look the part of a professor. "Do you mind walking me to the street?"

A STAR IN THE BLUE

No mummy jumped out at them or leaped from behind a car in the parking lot. Safe in his car, Leandro waved at Jones and drove off. Jones followed the hedge to the front of the museum where he had to weave through a third-grader fieldtrip. A flock of birds, a school of fish, boys and girls. One of them was anchored with a teacher next to his bicycle. The girl was crying. Her hand was attached to the handlebar.

"Hi," said Jones, "What's going on?"

The teacher recognized Jones. That wasn't so surprising, he was a regular feature in the *Herald*, and he had an ad in the yellow pages with his picture. "Look Peggy!" she said, "A detective is here!"

"This is my bike!" the girl sobbed.

"I don't know what we're going to do," Mrs. Ames told him. "She won't leave. We need to get the children inside the museum. You're sure this is your bike?"

"Yes! Someone stole it," the girl cried and she curled her arms around the frame in a tight hug. The planet was full of bicycles but only one of them was hers.

"Oh Jeeze…" Jones tipped his fedora back and scratched his head. What else could he do? What was the point of possessions anyway? Disparity. Whose idea was that to begin with? What's the point? We're only here for a moment, even the earth will one day turn out the light. But a child wouldn't grasp that, not yet. Getting her bicycle back was the only thing that mattered.

"Let me see if I can help." Jones kneeled next to the kickstand. He lifted the bike chain by the lock. "I've seen these before," he said, alternating spinning the dial numbers and holding the clicking to his ear, until "Presto!" the clasp unsnapped.

What a reaction Jones Jr. got. What joy!

This was all the mummy wanted too, to reunite with his princess after eons apart.

Mrs. Ames promised Peggy the bike would be safe on the school bus while they toured the museum. She and the girl wheeled it across the street and like the Lone Ranger, Jones slipped from sight.

He was counting on riding home when he was done, he was going to miss his bike, he was sad. The bike had served him well, they had been through a lot. Who could forget his clash with bicycle rustlers, or the time someone cut the brake line and Jones steered downhill into a hydrangea, or when someone tied tin cans to his fender with a sign that said Just Married. Jones liked the sea breeze and the way the colored straws in the spokes rattled like a tambourine. Now it looked like he was hoofing it. A long walk in the dark after a long day awaited him. Then again, maybe he could catch a ride from Hiphenou? That car he drove was one of those fast jobs. Fast enough to outrun a mummy and most other troubles. Jones crossed the street. He didn't have a destination in mind. Breakfast would be nice.

Someone else was missing breakfast too. This was the second morning the seagull on the trailer didn't get crusts. The gull wasn't happy about that.

Something had to be done about it. The seagull decided it needed to send a message, a very strong message to Jones Jr. It took off from the trailer and swung out over the beach, using the breeze to gain height, going up to where it would only be a little white star in the blue morning sky.

Jones had a handful of hours to kill before 2 o'clock. After some breakfast, he supposed he could look for Phil. He didn't figure it would be so easy to find him...but it only took ten minutes.

Five blocks away, a gorilla sat at the counter of Sunnyside Diner.

PHIL THE GORILLA

Phil's eyes burned in the mask. They were hunted, angry eyes. The slumped back was familiar, but not much else. He drank his hot coffee through a straw. There were crumbs in his fur. "I can't believe you sold me out," the gorilla seethed.

"I didn't sell you out, Phil. I didn't tell them where you live or where you might be or what you're trying to do with the Avalon you stole. For all they know I won't be able to find you."

The gorilla eyes glared at Jones.

"I promise, Phil."

At last, the gorilla sighed. "Okay. I'm glad to hear that. Thanks Jones. Sorry I expected the worst of you. I uhhh...I might have to apologize for something I did. On the spur of the moment. I—"

Jones interrupted, "They know you took their Avalon. They're going to get you. Forget the money, just give them back the box."

"I can't."

"Phil, they're from another planet or somewhere. Who knows what they can do?"

"I sold it."

Jones could only stare.

"I'm sick of the way things are," Phil said.

A waitress moving along the counter stopped in front of them. "More coffee, Mr. Talking Gorilla?"

"Oh sure. Thanks very much."

As soon as she was gone, Phil said, "Do you know what? I come here a lot and she never asks me if I want more coffee. I have to bend over backwards to get noticed. But I turn into a gorilla and suddenly I'm the toast of the town."

"It's inexplicable," said Jones. "Like you unloading all that Avalon."

"Not all of it. I saved a couple capsules." He reached for the floor and got the crumpled grocery bag. "Gorillas don't have pockets. Reach in there and take one. The other one's for me."

"I don't want it."

"Just do it, Jones. You never know. We run in dangerous circles. You might need to disappear in a hurry." He sipped his straw. "Do it, Jones. Take one."

So he did. He knew he would end up taking it. Thoughts of Avalon called him. It was like here but everything was better.

"That's good." The gorilla put the bag next to its feet again.

Jones said, "What am I supposed to tell the Avalon girl?"

"Simple. Just say you haven't seen me."

Jones was thinking.

The straw slurped.

Jones said, "What will happen to the Avalon you sold?"

"Dealer's got it. It'll go fast. I bet they're already gone."

"Whoever uses it goes to Avalon."

The gorilla nodded.

"I imagine some of them won't want to come back." Jones knew the feeling.

"It's nice there, right? You can't blame them."

Jones agreed, "Why'd you return?"

Phil thought about it. One day he saw someone vanish. It was just a normal day, Phil was on his way to the bookie, cutting through an alley and ahead of him he saw a man eat something and pop—gone. A magic trick. Phil was curious. Was there a trapdoor set in the bricks? No. He searched the spot. It was all solid reality. The only thing left behind was a small box full of the capsules that would set so many wheels in motion. He hurried back home instead and dared himself to open the box and take one of its capsules, only half of one, who knew what it would do, and instantly he was in Avalon, in a field of sunflowers made of diamonds and gold.

Phil sat at the counter of Sunnyside Diner, but he was also remembering Avalon. Avalon is going on all the time, right here, right now, you just can't see it. He snapped three of the tall stalks and clutched them, he would have grabbed more but they were heavy. When he was back in his apartment, he could break them up and hock the pieces. He could make a steady trade going from his apartment to Avalon until he was the richest man in America! Euphoria in Avalon. He loved it, but elation didn't last long. When the capsule wore out, he was in his room again. Emptyhanded. The gold and diamonds were gone but the box was there beside him. At least he still had that. That's when he wondered *How much can I get for that?* "I don't know," he answered Jones, "there must be something wrong with me."

The waitress heard that. Phil thought his voice was muffled by the fur and rubber, but she heard him as she passed, and she stopped and put her hand on his arm.

SHAKEDOWN ON SUNNYSIDE

Car tires screeched to the curb on Sunnyside, and doors whipped open and slammed. Shoe leather scuffed the concrete. "Phil Ticks…we been looking for you."

The gorilla froze. Jones just finished saying "see you later" to him there in front of the diner. When he saw Mr. Tee and Not Hardly approaching, he feared later would be a lot longer.

"I told you that's him," said Not Hardly.

Mr. Tee pointed at Jones, "Pathetic. You think you can give us the slip by changing your suit and wearing glasses?" He grabbed Jones by the arm. "What do you say we take you for a little ride?"

"Umm, I'd say no."

"Very funny, wise guy. Come with us."

"Now hold on a minute," Jones stalled. "My friend here is flush with cash. How much do you need? Two dimes?"

"Friend? I don't see no friend."

Jones turned around. "The gorilla I was with… Where'd he go?"

"Gorilla," Not Hardly said. "That's rich."

"Phil!" Jones called, glancing anxiously, but it was no use. Phil knew when to flee.

They each took a raincoat arm and propelled Jones towards the car. "Hold on! I'm not Phil Ticks."

Not Hardly shoved him across the back seat and sat next to him while Mr. Tee hustled around to the driver's side. Jones said, "You guys are making a mistake. I can prove it, I can show you my wallet, I'm not Phil Ticks."

"Zip it, Ticks."

"Yeah," Mr. Tee agreed. "It's about time you find out how serious this is." The car made a sharp turn and accelerated. "You can't hide from us, Ticks. We got you. You're gonna pay the hard way."

What a way to go, thought Jones. The dull

shapes of warehouses flashed by. "Fellahs—"

"Didn't I tell you to zip it?"

"Okay, okay, I'm zipping," Jones put his hand to his mouth and kept it there. The capsule Phil gave him was stuck to his palm. Avalon was always better, wasn't it?

THE CRIMSON TOPAZ

It didn't take Frida long to find Jones. An orange light was on inside his little house shining warmly onto the grassy plot where his Lincoln was parked. A big moon floated in the starry sky above. There were more stars than he'd ever seen. Jones was sitting on his porch, head leaned back absorbing outer space.

Frida left her bicyclebird next to the parked Continental. The wings came down and rested on the car metal. In a second she was beside him and in another second—everything jumped like a dream—they were next to a tall monument. She was telling him about it.

"All those people who took stolen Avalon don't want to leave. They'd rather die than go back. Look what we had to make for them."

Jones never saw a lighthouse quite like it. Stone was carved from a pool of water, up into the sky like the fin of a fish, and at the top, a hundred feet high, a blue candlelight shone. Inside the jagged flame, scenes were changing. A face appeared, Jones recognized a street, a stairway, a building in the rain, flickering views from America.

It reminded Jones of the factory smokestacks that dotted the skyline with clouds at home. "What's it doing?"

"Burning memories, all those people who took Avalon." Frida said.

A dim figure ran past them and leaped into the sinking blue water surrounding the stone.

"They're drawn to the light," she said. "That's all that matters to them."

"What's happening to them?"

"They're starting over. They're not ready for Avalon yet, they can't survive here, not the way they are."

"That's too sad," Jones said and averted his eyes. He wished he had a cigarette. This land didn't even have a 7-Eleven. Beyond the hill was another Pacific Ocean, one without pollution or shipwrecks, one that teemed with shimmering fish.

Frida touched his shoulder. "They'll be okay. Avalon will heal them. That other world where you're from was too much for them."

Jones nodded. "Sometimes I don't like it there, when I can't scrounge up enough for taxi fare, or I look at a newspaper headline, or just the general despair, but I'm not ready to trade it in. It's not all bad. In fact, I've grown to like it. Also, I wouldn't want to forget everything."

"You will eventually. You'll have to. Everyone starts here new."

Jones looked at the monument again. A last memory faded in the flame. He wasn't so sure about Avalon now.

"Look, a new citizen." Frida pointed.

From the candlelight a spark floated like a parachute. It soared over them, over the flowers shut down for the night. It turned a little and headed for the trees. Jones didn't know much about the geography of this world, but he recognized the mountains and the lay of the land. Once he flew that same route in a Pan Am jet, a thousand feet above the forest, gaining altitude to make it over the mountains, then staying level at eight miles on the way to the Great Lakes and beyond to the Atlantic Ocean. "Where are they going to land?"

"Who knows? It's up to Avalon."

The parachute spark got lost in the stars.

Frida said, "Why are you here? Are you going to join them? Do you feel the light pulling you?"

"No, definitely not. I just came here to get away from danger. It's probably safe to go back. I have things to do."

She smiled. "That's good."

"Only...I hate to bring this up..." His Avalon case wasn't exactly successful, but, "Back where I'm from we need money to survive. That two hundred dollars you gave me when you hired me..."

Suddenly it wasn't night anymore and they weren't at his beach house or at the memory monument, they were seated at a familiar taco stand on the pier.

"You spent it already?" Frida said.

"No, it disappeared. It went invisible as soon as you did."

She nodded, "I'm sorry, I should have known. Avalon things can't stay in your world."

He was holding a taco. A bite was taken out. "What about the box with all the Avalon capsules? How could that be kicking around?"

She shrugged. "I don't know. Some things can. Have you ever seen a hummingbird? Those are from here." She took a sip of Moxie. "Don't worry though, I'll figure out a way to repay you, and not in hummingbirds," she smiled.

He pictured bringing birds to the bank, putting them in his account.

"And what about expenses?" she asked.

"Oh, I took a couple taxis, I paid for Phil Ticks' breakfast, I lost my bicycle, but I don't think that counts."

She promised he would be compensated even if she had to tie twenties to a flock of western emeralds. He laughed at the thought of those radiant green humminbirds gliding into his trailer. She finished her meal and scooted from her chair. "Thanks for the taco."

"They're good, aren't they? It's funny that Casa Tacos has a branch here in Avalon. They really get around." He opened his wallet to find it full of tens and fives. He laughed. What could he possibly lack in Avalon? Apparently there are no hardships. And no lack of flowers and warm breeze.

There are 366 species of hummingbird. A crimson topaz sat on a blue lilac stem. The little bird looked at Jones. Could a hummingbird go back and forth between worlds and still carry memories here and there? Jones supposed they could.

"It's time for us to say goodbye," Frida said.

"I just wonder, can I ask a favor? I don't want to return to the same situation I was in. I was in a bit of a predicament. Can you direct me to another place and time?"

"That depends."

"Nothing exotic, I promise. It would be great if I could reappear in the museum at, say 1:45. I have an appointment there at 2. It would be a big help."

"Wait right there." Frida crossed the pier to what looked like a phonebooth and she dialed something.

The taco stand was gone. They were back in the field where he started. Avalon had a mind of its own.

She gave him a capsule. She said something that was worn away, just a sound like sandpaper on pine. Jones watched her pedal and fly away on her bicyclebird. It looked fun, but he thought if she gave him one of those contraptions to go back on, he would end up flapping over the boulevard like Icarus with melting pigeon wings. The capsule would be safer. That's what he thought.

JONES THE MAMMOTH

Jones Jr. may be the first human to materialize inside of a mammoth. He was caught in the cage of its skeleton, while only inches away a sabertooth tiger skull opened its mouth to eat him. For a few seconds Jones feared that Frida's Avalon sent him a lot further than 1:45 PM. Did her finger slip in the phonebooth and accidentally set his capsule for 15,000 years ago? Then he became aware of kids shouting, marble pillars, wooden walls cluttered with paintings, and he knew he was in the museum.

He recognized the main entrance hall. Footsteps ran towards the railing that ran a circle around the prehistoric cemetery he was displayed in. Jones wondered if Avalon did this to him on purpose. Fortunately, there was just enough room between the two sides of mammoth ribs for him to wriggle free. His escape certainly didn't go unnoticed.

He bustled through his audience. The last thing he wanted to do was answer questions or sign autographs. A detective like William Conrad's Frank Cannon would have rolled right out of there to his signature Lincoln Continental, but Jones lost his car quite a while ago and Violet Zen was calling his name.

"Jones! Jones, it's me!"

He kept shuffling for the door labeled **To 1st Floor**. She caught up with him and slowed him down. "That was incredible, Jones. Are you a magician now? That's it, right? Jones Jr. the Magic Detective! Oh, I have to get your picture for the *Herald*."

"Sorry," he grunted as he pulled away, "Not a chance."

"There's always a chance!" Violet called after him. She quickly took a shot of him with her camera. His back, fedora, raincoat flapping, clown pants. The photo will appear in tomorrow's paper with her column. **Jones Jr., a soft-boiled** detective if ever there was one, wowed a crowd at the museum yesterday, presenting his new talent—magic.

The stairway echoed with sneakers and his hurried breathing. Zen wasn't after him, it was just the sound of himself. He opened the next door and nearly tumbled into the first-floor hallway.

For Leandro Hiphenou, already on edge, all that commotion sounded like the mummy's revenge. He peeked from his room ever so carefully. If he saw the creature, he had a book of matches in his hand, he was ready to set that ancient papyrus husk on fire like Lon Chaney in *The Mummy's Tomb*.

It was okay, they were relieved to see each other. Jones didn't want to admit he crawled out of a mammoth, and Hiphenou, on the run since leaving his lecture hall, quickly put his mummy matches away as he opened the office door.

"I need to sit down a minute," Jones croaked.

"Of course. That mummy's made me a nervous wreck too."

"I'll be okay. I just have to catch my breath." Jones was discouraged that's all it took to tire him. When he was young, he could have wrestled that saber-tooth to the ground, or if not that, run from it a lot faster. The years were wearing him out. In 15,000 more years, he could be a skeleton in a museum too, held down by Avalon.

Leandro had hidden the can of tana leaves in a big hollow book. If this was one of his precious mummy movies, the camera would zoom in as he flipped open the cover of a Mediterranean cookbook and removed the tin can inside. He stretched his hands in front of himself, like a plutonium janitor, as he carried the can to the hotplate under the window. A pan of water was waiting. "It is said that during the cycle of the moon, the tana leaves fluid can be administered to a mummy to bring it to life. I did that. I regret it. There's also a scene in every mummy movie where the High Priest of Cairo looks into the boiling tana potion steam and can see the past happening. That's what we need to do." He filled the pan with leaves and switched the hotplate on. "We need to know the past to know what we're up against."

Jones' walkie-talkie squawked. He held it to his ear and pressed the talk button. "This is Jones."

After five seconds, Roscoe said, "You didn't say over. Over"

"For crying out loud!" Jones steamed, "Not

that again!" then added a forceful, "Over."

"Just checking on you. Over."

"I'm fine, we're just boiling some tana leaves."

"…Over?"

"Yes, over!"

The robot continued, "I wanted to alert you there's a 10-76 at the museum. Over."

"Can you just tell me what that means without the number? Over."

"A trespasser crawled out of a Paleolithic skeleton and is currently active in your vicinity."

"That was me, Roscoe! Over." Then Jones pressed the button again, "Is there really a number for that?" and "Over."

"Stay on your toes, Jones," the robot warned. "Over and out."

"We're starting to get a picture," Hiphenou said.

Jones got to his feet. He felt a little dizzy.

Hiphenou was leaning over the pan, the steam was clouding out and spiriting up along the glass, out the open window.

"What do you see?" said Jones.

"It's most remarkable. I see pyramids, the pharaoh, the Nile, crocodiles. Look, see for yourself. See the hieroglyphics? Look, we're in the temple, the priest is preparing tana leaves too."

Jones removed his fake glasses, they were all steamed up. All he could see was smoke.

The pot bubbled and Leandro continued his narrative. A thick plume was headed out the window.

"There's the princess," Leandro said. "The devoted mummy will search the world over to find her reincarnation."

Jones put his glasses on and everything was plain as day as he stared at the princess in the boiling tana leaves transmission. "I know her," he nearly said. He didn't get a chance to say her name.

Above them, the mummy filled the window frame.

MOON TECHNOLOGY

What happens when a mummy goes berserk on tana leaf smog? Hiphenou's office was kneedeep in torn books and paper and broken furniture and glass. The unfortunate Egyptologist was buried under a bookshelf. The cooking pan was gone and the office had the unquiet silence of a room after a bomb.

Akhenaten's face slid from a pile of rubble as the book was pushed aside. Slowly, Jones emerged from the rubble and leaned against the scarred wallpaper. A big silver crack ran across the room. It was gone when he took off his bent glasses. "Professor?" Hiphenou's desk had been cleaved in half. There was no sign of him.

Jones reached into his rain jacket and got his walkie-talkie. A battery fell out of it. He let the rest of the smashed contraption fall. What a mess. It was worse than when he crawled from his crashed Lincoln Continental. As he raised his tennis shoe from the debris, the heap began to slide and he rocked his arms to regain his balance. Right away he slipped again as he jumped away from a snake. The black coils wound through the New Kingdom books. Then his detective senses took over and identified it as a telephone cord. Of course.

Someone was going to need a wheelbarrow to clear the room. Jones followed the cord. He imagined the crackpot conversation he was going to have when he called the police. "I'd like to report a follow-up on that 10-76 at the museum." And how would they take it when they found out about the mammoth?

The telephone must have been thrown off the desk. Those flailing mummy arms knocked both Jones and Hiphenou aside and buried them alive as it whirlwinded around the walls. Jones gave the cord a pull and freed it from under a chair. He wouldn't have to make that phone call. The wire had been snapped.

It occurred to Jones at this point it didn't look good for him to stick around. That's putting it lightly.

A gray giant stood in the broken window.

This time Jones did lose his balance. The haunted pharaoh was back, Jones was doomed.

"Relax." It was a robot voice. "I figured you'd need backup."

"Roscoe, do you have to sneak up like that? Wait—how'd you get here?"

"I'll show you. We should vacate the premises now."

"I don't know where the professor is."

Roscoe said, "Under those books. He'll be fine. We don't have time, you have to hurry."

Jones got up on the counter where the hotplate was. The air still smoldered. The robot lent him a metal claw to steady him outside. Birds were singing again. They weren't scared for long—seen one mummy break into a museum, seen them all—they were up in all the branches sending telegrams as the whine of police sirens grew.

The mummy had left a trail of trampled hedge.

"Over there." Roscoe strode top speed, clanking like a peach can filled with loose change.

On the grass median between the museum and the next stone building, it seemed the janitor left two garbage cans, but Jones didn't see any quick mode of transportation. "Where?"

Roscoe didn't answer him, he was aimed where they had to go. Twenty paces ahead, Roscoe stopped at a garbage can and opened a door. He scooted through and shut himself inside. "Get in yours."

The sirens were getting louder. Jones quickly obeyed. A detective was no stranger to garbage cans. Once Jones spent a whole night in one, watching through binoculars.

Roscoe said, "Press the green button."

Imagine a duet for two vacuum cleaners.

"Hold on tight." Roscoe directed them into the air. Soon, the museum was no bigger than a sand castle.

"What are these things?" Jones felt like he was being carried in a beach bucket floating along beside Roscoe.

"It's moon technology."

"I see." Jones held a hand on his fedora. "And you've had them for how long?"

"A year or two."

"Are you telling me I could have used this instead of that kid's bike?"

Rosco was silent. He was occupied with the controls of their flying machines.

"Wait a second, Roscoe! How did you get out of the trailer?"

PARADISE COVE

They kicked up dust and sand as they landed in the parking lot at Paradise Cove. The vacuum cleaner whir stopped.

"Did you make these?" Jones departed it, glad to be back on the ground. For all anyone could tell, it was a garbage can again. "From directions? Did you get directions from the Moon?"

"I got the plans from a comic book."

"Really? Gee, they sell anything in those." Jones was going to tell Roscoe something else, but he was distracted. A message was spraypainted on the side of his trailer.

"I forgot to tell you about that," said Roscoe.

Jones read it aloud, "JJ is a snitch." It looked like a 6th grader wrote it.

"10-12. Vandalizing."

"Thanks Roscoe."

"It's not good for our business."

"Yeah. I know that, Roscoe. I'll paint over it after I get something to eat. I've had a rough day." His tennis shoes panted up the wooden steps to the screen door. "Aww, forget it, let's go down to the pier for tacos." A memory of Avalon.

Jones ordered six tacos. After the first three, he went to get another root beer and he told the girl at the counter, "Esto es major que un sueño." She was at Casa Tacos five days a week, 11-8, not counting cleanup and prep for the next day. If this was a dream, it was his, not hers. But she smiled.

Jones saved a last bite from his last taco for the seagull that lived on his roof. He wrapped the silky checkerboard paper around that morsel and put it in his raincoat. He tried to do that whenever he had leftovers. He tossed them up on the rusted roof like chum. It shouldn't take the gull long to swoop down.

The sun pushed shadows ahead of them on the pier. Roscoe helpfully advised the people leaning on the handrail with reels where it was best to fish from, regarding current and tide. Before they reached land, Jones looked over his shoulder. Nobody had moved. They didn't care what a robot thought.

You couldn't approach the trailer without reading the words painted on it. Jones sent his eyes up to the rooftop. The gull wasn't there. He got the crumpled morsel from his pocket, ready to throw. "Know what, Roscoe? I think I'll wait until the morning to paint. What's the point? It will be dark soon."

"If you say so."

Once in a while Jones could catch something almost human in the robot's tone. Jones knew what the robot was thinking: why leave for tomorrow what you can do today, etc. The poor metal man never learned to take it easy when you got the chance.

Jones skyhooked the taco bite onto the flat roof before he opened the trailer door. It was too bad the seagull wasn't there. It was too bad its thirst for revenge took it from Paradise Cove into the stratosphere.

"There's my chair!" Jones rejoiced as he made

it around the desk and onto the red leather.

When he opened his eyes, Roscoe was still in view, outside at the base of the stairs. Jones sat up, "Say, how did you get through that doorway?"

Roscoe clopped out of the frame. In a moment he began to unzip the wall. Daylight showed in the seam, up, across, and down. A perfect ramp shape separated from the trailer and lowered like a drawbridge.

"Isn't that something," Jones marveled.

Roscoe climbed into the trailer and resealed the wall and shut the door.

"I'm really impressed." He got a cigarette. "Plus, you made those crazy moon machines. You're ingenious, I mean it. I think you need a *Popular Mechanics* feature story." At least he could tell Zen, she'd love it. Jones was about to light the cigarette when someone knocked on the door. Jones looked at Roscoe and shrugged. It was going on evening, he wanted done with adventure for the day. Whatever it was, he hoped it wasn't mummy related. He got up and asked the door, "Who is it?"

"Zahra."

"Zahra!" he repeated. She was the princess he

saw in the tana leaves. He swept the door open, "Come in, quick." He looked around her. Parked cars, a sunburned family looking for their station wagon. He pressed her soft shoulder.

"What's the matter, Jones?"

"Come here, Zahra. Have a seat. I have to tell you something."

She sat opposite him. "Is it about what was painted outside?

"No, that's a…misunderstanding. I have a pretty good idea who did it. A gorilla. He apologized, but notice he's not over here painting over it."

"Well, it's fixed now," she said with a smile.

Jones was confused.

"Can I show you?" she said.

She looked so pleased with herself, how could he say no?

Zahra moved in one excited ibis swoop to the door. He had seen her starring in a hotplate pan, beginning in white Egyptian linen, performing a thousand reincarnations to this century. Jones took a little longer to get from the desk to the door.

It was just before dusk, the golden hour when sunlight poured like syrup over Paradise Cove. The sound of waves and kids and distant transistor radios.

She was smiling next to the graffiti.

He had important news to tell her about the mummy that had risen from the land of the dead and was looking for her, but for now he was happy to laugh at her punctuation, how she added two letters and an apostrophe with her black paintbrush and changed the message into: JJ isn't a snitch.

SMUGGLERS AT MIDNIGHT

Jones wasn't sure if Zahra took his warning to heart. He could only hope she would think about it. There's no easy way to tell someone a mummified pharaoh is after you. Roscoe didn't have a police code for that. That code has been forgotten for millenniums. Perhaps it would be revealed in a Hiphenou lecture, when the police rode the cobblestone streets on mechanical camels and the dispatcher read the Scroll of Thoth over the airwaves.

The parking lot gate was locked for the night. The trailer windows were open. Crickets were telegraphing. If a mummy came following Zahra's trail, scratching through the weeds, they would let Jones know with a deathly silence. And Jones would hear it shuffle across the tar.

The Case of the Avalon Box was concluded, but not really—he still had those two hoodlums after him, thinking he was Phil Ticks. How was he going to shake them? That's what he was working on. Jones leaned over the table painting a declaration in bold letters on the front of a t-shirt. It was a newspaper headline, dramatic, with a hint of mystery. "How's this?" He held it up so Roscoe could read it.

The robot recited, "I'm not Phil Ticks."

Jones grinned, "What do you think?"

"Do you expect your assailants to see that and leave you alone?"

"Well, yeah." He lay it flat again to dry.

The telephone rang.

Jones' hand jumped like a frog across the table towards it. "Hello?"

"Detective Jones?"

"That's me."

"It's Professor Hiphenou."

"There you are! How're you doing?"

"I'm in the hospital."

"Oh, that's too bad. What happened?"

"They tell me I'm in fair condition. Ironically though, I'm wrapped up like that mummy."

"Gee, I'm sorry to hear that."

"The nurse very kindly brought me the telephone so I could see if you made any progress."

"You know, I have actually." Jones told him about Zahra, how her dark eyes widened at his warning, how she probably decided Jones was just another kook—how could she not?—and how she left into the night.

"You fool!" Hiphenou wheezed. "It's just like Zita Johann in the 1932 mummy movie! You can't just let her wander off. She's a reincarnated princess! The mummy always lurks about at night. It's nighttime now, she's in danger!"

"Oh, she'll be fine."

Hiphenou groaned.

Jones said, "Listen, I don't even know where she lives."

"Don't you have a telephone book?"

"Sure I do, but all I know is her first name."

"What am I paying you for, Jones? You didn't stop the mummy from wrecking my office and knocking me around. My life is in ruins. I don't know if the mummy is coming back for more. And you won't even protect the—the—" his tirade was sidetracked by the steady increasing tone of a hospital monitor beeping more and more shrill.

"Easy, professor," said Jones. "I gave her my card. If she needs to, she'll call me. I can be there in two minutes in a flying garbage can."

"I'm sorry, sir." A woman's voice addressed Jones. "The patient needs to rest. You can speak tomorrow during visitor hours. Goodnight."

Jones hung up. "Alright," he sighed, "Now do I need to worry all night about Zahra?"

He listened to the crickets.

Roscoe was silent.

Jones wondered: When Roscoe was this desolate way, were there crickets in his head too?

"I think I'll go take a walk. Let me know if you hear anything." Jones left the table, ten steps from the door, "Oh, that's right. My walkie-talkie is kaput. Do we have any more of those?"

"No. I can make you something. It could be ready by morning."

"Okay, yeah, that would be great. I'll see you Roscoe, I'll be back soon." He opened the door and the night swept in. Nothing beat that ocean breeze. He left the light pooled around the trailer and headed for the shore.

The tar became the tamped path, soft sand, beachgrass flicked against him. Then he stopped and balanced, first one leg then the other, as he carefully removed his shoes. The sand got softer and cool as water. It felt good to dig toes into it. Mummies, gangsters, Avalon…he could burrow deep into this sand and be happy as a clam.

The ocean came into wide view. He left the cover of the reeds, onto the end of America, sand that dipped into the Pacific and washed from sight. Viewed from the sea, the beach was also the doorstep of America. Opportunity and untold riches awaited the submarine visitor who came ashore.

Some nights he would bring the folding chair. The mighty roar of the rollers sending water in and withdrawing, over and over. Tonight he was headed for any old dune, it didn't matter.

There was only one problem. The shape of a black boat had landed in the surf and silhouettes were coming and going. They were trotting up to the shadows cloaking the rocky cliff. Jones knew where they were going, carrying boxes into a cave, and he knew what they were: smugglers.

"Forget it," he growled, "I can't handle another mystery."

NEBRASKA POSTCARD

"It's time to open the gate," Roscoe told him.

Jones had no idea what he'd been dreaming and didn't care. As long as he woke up, he was ready to start over. He left the bed and put on his plaid bathrobe. "Thanks Roscoe."

With a little wiggling, he slipped his feet into his sneakers. He didn't have far to go but once he stepped on a diamond of broken glass in the parking lot. That was no fun. "Say Roscoe," he turned in the doorway, "Would you mind making some coffee?"

"10-4."

Jones grinned. He knew that one.

Another sunny day beginning.

The ocean, birds, the flop of his sneakers on the tar, up a gentle incline to the gateway. Jones unlocked the chains, separated them and strung them into the weeds, coiling them on each side of the paving. What a setup. A trailer in Paradise Cove. After breakfast he would sweep and pick up any trash and make sure the parking lot was a postcard you could mail to Nebraska and write: Wish you were here.

SPHINX AT THE WINDOW

Two garbage cans landed on the sidewalk. The whine of their engines settled with the dust they raised. Jones was worried when their flight took them low, clipped a maple tree limb coming in under the telephone wires. He wished there was another way to get around. He missed that Lincoln Continental.

"This is her house," Roscoe said.

He had to hand it to him, all Jones had to do was tell the robot Zahra's name and in just a little buzzing while, Roscoe figured out where she lived. Flying phonebook wasn't all Roscoe was capable of—more and more Jones was discovering how underappreciated his metal friend was. For instance, after the beach was open for business and Jones returned to the trailer for coffee, he asked Roscoe about a walkie-talkie replacement.

"It's right there before you," Roscoe had told him.

"What? All I see if a cup of coffee." Was he supposed to hold it to his ear like a seashell?

"Next to the sugar."

Jones leaned forward. There was an ant meandering around the sugar bowl. Jones squinted through his glasses. Was it possible? Did that tiny creature have a miniature walkie-talkie? What an incredible invention, Jones marveled, he could carry that ant on his coat lapel and nobody would know he was secretly in communication with a robot in a trailer miles away.

"It's the watch," said Roscoe.

"The ant is wearing a watch?"

"What ant? Look at the wristwatch next to the sugar."

"Ohhh." Jones picked it up. The silver face of it had a clock, a speaker, and four little buttons on the edge. "Say, this is nice."

"It's a two-way radio."

Yes indeed. Roscoe was amazing.

As Jones stepped out of his garbage can in front of Zahra's house, he checked his new watch. The trip took three minutes, a song in a jukebox, to arrive. Not bad. He was also wearing his yellow seersucker suit again. He was done with disguises. On the way up the path to the door, he picked a bluebell flower for his coat buttonhole. A sleepy bumblebee sat on the flagstone like a lump of fudge, going nowhere. He didn't share Hiphenou's panic for Zahra, this was a pleasant scene, birds in the camelia tree, he and Roscoe were just paying her a friendly visit making sure.

A yellow cat sat on the back of a chair in the window. Its golden eyes stared at Jones. The posture made Jones think of a sphinx. What if it was guarding Zahra's door? Jones was terrible at riddles, his mind just didn't work that way. If that was a sphinx Jones would be sure to end up another skeleton tossed on a pyramid pile. Before the creature could open its mouth, Jones took a couple steps backwards, right into Roscoe. "Ouch!" he winced.

The picture in the window changed. The cat was gone. Zahra waved at them and left the curtain swishing. In a moment she opened the door and called, "More strange visitors!" The cat brushed around her bare ankles. "You were right about the mummy," she told Jones.

"It's here?"

"No, not quite. Will you come inside?"

"Sure," said Jones.

"I'll be fine here," Roscoe said. He preferred a door with a zipper. He stood like a birdbath in the yard. The sand-colored cat went out to investigate him.

Jones was ready for her room to be a shambles like the office in the museum, but that wasn't the case. Nothing had been thrown around, books were in their place, paintings on the wall, there was even an untipped vase of long stem roses.

"Have a seat," she said. "What's that say on your shirt?"

Jones opened the yellow coat to show all the t-shirt words.

She read, "I Am Not Phil Ticks."

"I've been having some trouble with mistaken identity," he explained. "I also taped a sign on my back, but it blew off on the way here."

It drifted from the flying garbage can and floated to the ground somewhere in the city below.

For a while it sat in the crown of a chestnut tree.

"What happened with the mummy?" he asked.

"It's okay now, it's all over." She told Jones it was just dawn when the mummy appeared in her house. He opened a window right there in the air in the middle of the room. She saw Egypt behind him, a sunny marble city fed by a river, pools and canals and lush gardens full of flowers, avenues lined by palm trees, graceful swanlike boats in the harbor, gliding machines flapping wings, all watched over by pyramids. It was beautiful but she didn't need another world. She said no.

Jones said he understood. It sounded like Avalon to him.

It broke the mummy's heart when she said no.

"That's what's left of him." Zahra pointed at a pile of bandages and dust. "I don't know if the museum wants him back." That was it, the end of the mummy caper.

COUNTERFEIT ATMOSPHERE

A few days passed. Jones settled back to his routine, caring for the parking lot. He raked the sand. He picked up trash. He unlocked the chain in the morning and locked it up at night. A simple life. One lazy afternoon while he was reading the *Herald* in the trailer shade, about ten minutes away from taking a nap, Roscoe called him. Jones lifted his wrist and answered, "Yeah."

"There's something on television you should see."

"What is it?"

"Just trust me." Roscoe didn't bother with 'over' anymore. It was a tired act that ran its course and was led out to pasture and left forgotten among the weeds like an abandoned tractor.

"Alright. I'll be there." With a wheeze he got out of his hammock. In back of the trailer was a fenced-in patio. Some flowers dried in pots. The sigh of waves past the slats. He shuffled to the doorway and pushed aside the curtain sheet.

The TV screen was clear as a polished tidepool.

"Wow!" said Jones, "How'd you get that picture?"

"Oh, just lucky, there must be something atmospheric today."

"Hold on, it's in color too!"

"Yes, the commercials are, but the film is black and white."

"But—"

"Here comes the program." Roscoe held up a claw to hush him.

A man onscreen in a shiny polyester shirt, slick rust hair, stared into the lens. "Welcome back." The camera retreated some to reveal the cheap set he was sitting in front of. Painted on the paneling behind him was Red's Matinee Movie, with a clock tower pointed at 1. "I'm Red, your host and owner of Red's Tavern on Lake City Way. With us today is," he read from a card, "Lendo—sorry if I get this wrong—Hipponoo. You're from the museum, right?"

The camera tagged to the left.

"Hiphenou. Leandro Hiphenou." He was awkwardly propped in an armchair. He was wrapped in gauze.

"What?" Jones gasped. Poor Hiphenou had become a mummy!

"You want to tell our viewers what happened to you?" said Red. "In case someone's been living under a log."

Leandro took a deep breath. Behind the bandages the words formed. "I'm an archaeologist, Egyptologist to be precise, that's my field of study. And yes, I work at the museum. I'm no stranger to the reliquaries and—"

Red grew impatient, "You got attacked by a mummy, right?"

"Yes. Yes, yes as you say, that is what happened."

"Looks like he did a number on you too." Red chuckled. "I think if I was there, I'da like to put up a fight." He punched the air, close to the potted fern between their chairs.

"I'm a scientist, sir. I have no intention of brawling with my subject matter."

"First of all, no mummy's gonna get a jump on me!" Red huffed.

"I was busied with a rather specific chemical reaction, an experiment, my attention was hardly inviting violent intrusion."

"One to the gut, one to the jaw," Red pantomimed. "Game over."

"Okay Red, congratulations, you've proved yourself. You're a better man than I."

Red smirked at the camera, "Let's get back to the movie."

The TV turned into a grainy Lou Costello shaking a candle inside a pyramid.

Steadily the screen was eaten by static, a steady flow of it like sand in an hourglass. "There goes the picture," said the robot. "We lost it."

"Just as well," said Jones. "Red hasn't changed." Jones met Red before, on a case by the docks. He was the same way at the harbor with the crew of a trawler. "He's a lousy detective too. Did I ever tell you about the time he tried to take credit for busting that smuggling operation?"

"Yes."

"The nerve of that guy." Jones heard the stories. Once in a while Phil did some gambling at Red's

Tavern. Jones used to drive past there at night when cars would fill the dark parking lot. A red neon name shined in the curtained window. Jones missed driving behind the wheel of a Lincoln Continental on Lake City Way, surrounded by spaceship lights, gas stations, fast-food restaurants.

There was a knock on the trailer door and Jones' first thought was: it's Red.

It wasn't.

"Are you there, Jones?" It was Frida. Her time away from Avalon was running out, she landed about half a mile down the beach and had to hurry to Paradise Cove.

"Hi, nice to see you." He showed her into the trailer to the table. "Have a seat. Can I get you some coffee?"

"No thanks. I'm not sure how long I have, Jones. I brought you something from Avalon." It was the same kind of box that had all the capsules. "I wanted to see if I could sneak something out of Avalon this way. And look, it worked." She opened the lid and got a stack of money and handed it to him. "This is a test to make sure it won't evaporate like last time."

"Is that Avalon money?"

"No, we don't have money. I made this in Avalon."

"Counterfeit?"

"No, it's an exact replica."

"Well, that's very nice, thank you."

She was going to say something more. He could tell she was about to. Then she wasn't there to say it.

That Avalon travel still surprised Jones. Pop! And he held a roll of tens and twenties. When was the last time he held that kind of money? He looked like he had robbed an armored car.

Roscoe alerted him, "She teleported."

"I know, but look what she gave us." Jones brought it to the cupboard and stashed it in the empty coffee can vault. He wondered what she wanted to tell him. "Actually, I'll take some of this to Thrifty. I'll get something good for dinner. You want anything?"

"From Thrifty?"

"Sure."

Roscoe sighed and thought about it. "Okay… Some oil."

THE CHLOROFORM AFFAIR

Jones leaned to the gray floor of his flying machine and removed a crushed Moxie can. That wasn't an unusual occurrence when you flew around in, landed, and left what looked like a garbage pail. Despite that, he was pleased. The Avalon money worked. He successfully bought a tin of chili, some orange juice, and oil for Roscoe. In return he got some genuine American currency for change. Even if his twenty vanished into their register till, Jones came out ahead.

He held onto the rim of the flying can with one hand and clutched a paper grocery bag in the other and calmly told the machine, "Take me back home."

The can lifted gently off the cement, buzzing over the shoppers who stopped on their way back to cars, humming past the big Thrifty sign and the telephone wires, a hundred feet off the ground in the lower reaches of the sky. He was in the birds' neighborhood.

As the crow flies, so did Jones go, avoiding the roads and traffic signs, out to the sea and along the shoreline. One of these times, he wanted to say "Take me to Japan" or "Let's go to Madagascar." What would happen? Adventure! What a way to see the world.

Below was the road he rode his bike on only a week ago. It strung along from town brushing the cliffsides and slopes. How many people in cars or walking along were looking up at a flying garbage can? The Paradise Cove parking lot was full of toylike vehicles. The trailer was a rivet rusted to the tar, getting bigger as Jones descended.

He became concerned as soon as he saw the black car parked next to his home and the two men who shaded their eyes staring at the bright sky and the approaching vacuum cleaner drone. "Oh no..." Jones knew the black car and he recognized Mr. Tee and Not Hardly. The can directed itself to the ground to a place right next to the other one. "Oh no...." A pair of shiny tin legs stuck out of the other garbage can, feet like flowers.

Soon as the contraption settled, Jones bolted out the door before the engine died. "Oh no... Roscoe, can you hear me?" He pulled on his friend's metal feet.

"He can't hear you."

"He's swimming with the fishes."

Jones turned on the two hoods behind him. "Why'd you take it out on him? He didn't do anything."

"Listen, Ticks. You—"

"No, you listen!" Jones barked at Mr. Tee. "For the last time, I'm not Phil Ticks! I never was, I never will be. He's just someone I know. I wouldn't even call him a friend, but he needed help—remember the Golden Rule? Help sounded easy enough, he wanted me to watch his shoeshine stand. I didn't know I'd get mixed up in some vengeance plot. My name's Jones. I live here, I'm the JJ painted on the trailer for all to see. Look—" They bristled as he reached into his coat and got his wallet. Five dollars and 43 cents, a punch-card for The Last Exit coffeehouse, his investigator's license, and his driver's ID. "Look—Jones Jr.—that's who I am!"

They looked at his cards and passed them back silently.

"Where is he?"

"How would I know? And even if I did, read the writing on the wall, I'm no snitch."

Not Hardly seized Jones by the arm. "We ain't leaving without some money. Ticks owes us. You know him, you're all we got, you pay us and we leave you alone."

"Pay you? Do you think I'm anything but poor? Do you think I'm crazy enough to throw away what little I have on horses and cards? Look at my trailer. Do you think that's a Carnegie library?"

"Pay up, or you end up in the other garbage can doing a headstand."

"Pushing up daisies," Mr. Tee growled.

"Fine! I'll give you all I have! Here!" he dumped the change out of his wallet. "And oh yes, there's more inside, come on follow me to the vault." He led them up the steps into the trailer, to the sink and the cupboard above it, swung open the hatch and got a can of coffee plugged with Avalon money. "Here! You've done it, what a heist. You got it all. I don't have a penny more."

They took it. Jones stood there pale, holding onto the sink, breathing hard. His heart was about to blow a valve. He shut his eyes like a knocked out chloroformed casualty. If he could have gone back to Avalon he might have. He waited until they left the trailer, banged the front door, got in their car, started the engine, gunned it and peeled away. Then Jones opened his eyes.

He could hear another car starting, taking someone's day at the beach home. Like listening to a seashell, the spell of the sea would whisper on. Jones headed for the door.

A vase of tin tulips waited outside.

"Oh Roscoe…"

The unlucky robot couldn't be pulled feetfirst from the can, Jones had to push his shoulder against it and tip it over. A mighty tugboat crash shook the ground. From the sound, Jones feared the can would be filled with nothing but scrap metal, but a woeful moan echoed out.

"Roscoe, you okay?" Jones got a hold of the robot's feet and heaved. "I'll get you out of there."

Yeah right. Jones needed the strength of four teenagers he recruited from the parking lot.

INSPECTOR CANARY

Roscoe was standing again. What a relief. He survived, with some new dents and a bit of a limp as he wobbled after Jones.

"I think we finally got rid of Phil's gangsters, Rosco. It cost us all our Avalon money though. Oh well, easy come, easy go." Jones stopped at the trailer door and reached into the mailbox. Nothing. It was empty as his wallet. He was standing on that last step, about to bring his groceries inside, when he heard his name called from the parking lot.

It was Reggie Canard, ex-jailbird. Jones knew him before he went to do time.

"Hey Canary."

"Please, Jones. In front of the kids, I'm

Inspector Canard." He turned to his flock. "Listen up, Junior Detectives. Wait here, I'll be right back." He left them waiting out of earshot to whisper, "This is my penalty. I have to do a little community service. The law's got me hitched to these know-it-alls. They want me to get the picture loud and clear that crime don't pay."

Jones said, "Solving crime doesn't pay either."

"Hey, I saw you at the bus station the other morning. You a shoe man now?"

"What?"

"I thought you were a cop."

"No, I'm a detective. I still am."

"Why you shining then? You a fence?"

"I'm not, no. I was just helping a friend."

"Alright," Canary shrugged. "I guess that's good."

Jones wondered if Phil had gone back to the depot, shining shoes in a gorilla suit. He had to make a living somehow. That disguise might even help business, the way an organ grinder will play music for a monkey holding a cup.

"Hey, Jones. I was thinking, what with me having the Junior Detectives, and you being a cop, or detective and all, can you let us in on anything shady around here? You know, for the boys and girls to investigate?"

"Ummm."

"I told them about your robot there, how it can decode the police radio. They just want to find some clues or whatever."

Roscoe said, "10-31."

"What's that?" Canary asked Jones, "What's he mean?"

Roscoe said, "Smuggling operation."

"Sure," said Jones, "That's right, I saw some smugglers the other night. Down on the beach, off to the right at the cliff."

"That's perfect!"

"I think there might be a trick wall. You better be careful. I saw them bringing lots of boxes inside a cave."

"I wonder if it's anyone I know."

"I don't want to know, Canary. Don't tell me anything about it. I'm taking a break, I'm not looking for any more trouble."

"Well, you know me, Jones. Trouble's my middle name. I'll see you later, and thanks pal," he shook Roscoe's claw, "We'll see if the Junior Detectives can uncover that smuggling operation."

Jones and Roscoe watched Canary and his troupe march in a line towards the beach. Bright and sure of themselves. Jones said quietly, "I thought I was the hero of this story, this life that wheels around me. I used to think I was really something special. I thought my reward would come naturally from being noticed, that it was right around the corner for me. Like prosperity."

DREAMING OF AVALON

Another week passed. Jones was getting to know the hammock, or the hammock was getting to know him. Even when he was out of it, the hammock held his shape imprinted in the webbing. It was spring and the bad weather was over and he only wanted to read Raymond Chandler and Dashiell Hammett library books.

Roscoe unzipped the trailer wall and stepped onto the patio with him.

Jones opened his eyes. *Red Harvest* was tented under his hands. He mumbled, "I'm not sleeping, Roscoe."

"You got a letter."

Jones sat up.

Roscoe delivered it. "Don't worry, it's okay. I read it."

The letter was taped and torn. Jones guessed Roscoe did that with his claws, but there was a white sticker on it that explained: **RETURNED FOR ADD'L POSTAGE.** It had gone back and forth from Avalon a couple times. "They must have had some trouble with the stamps."

Roscoe said, "That's what I thought too."

The envelope's return address claimed it had been mailed from The Avalon Embassy, Wilshire Boulevard, Los Angeles, California. But who knew what to believe? Jones looked at Roscoe. "Is it good news?"

"Find out."

That's what a detective is supposed to do. He ripped a corner and pulled on the tape strip. "Is this mummy approved?"

"It's from Frida," Roscoe said. He couldn't stand the suspense.

"Really?" Jones turned the envelope. There was so much tape on it, it was a real struggle to retrieve the letter inside. "Jeeze, how did you manage to read it?"

Roscoe pointed a claw at his electric eye.

"Right. X-ray spectacles. Hang on—here it comes." Using two fingers like a robot claw, Jones gripped the edge of the letter and pulled it through. "I hope this was worth the effort." He unfolded it. It caught the sunshine and glared. "Oh no, where are my glasses?"

Roscoe said, "They're on top your head."

With the world in focus, Jones exclaimed, "Look at this writing, it's like calligraphy." His own writing resembled the trail of a woodworm. He also noticed the small gray and white shell scotch taped at the bottom of the letter. With so much Egypt on his mind, he thought it might be a scarab.

"It's a sunflower seed," Roscoe informed him.

"Yes," Jones agreed. He couldn't get over her pretty writing, words moved like birds, the way geese will float across a white morning sky. "Frida says the money she gave us reappeared back in Avalon. That didn't take very long, did it? I guess it's not surprising. It's the same way you can't bring something out of a dream. Believe me, I've tried. It won't work. I guess you wouldn't know about dreams, would you Roscoe? Or do you?" Maybe there was something in Senior's cardboard box for that. Presenting Roscoe II, the dreaming robot. Jones returned to the letter. "She says: I'm sending you something else instead, an Avalon sunflower seed. See if this can grow."

That was the end of the letter. It went the way everything from Avalon did—gone with a pop. But Jones caught the sunflower seed as it fell from the air. It was small enough to hide another world in its shell.

It would grow in a red clay pot along the side of the metal trailer. The sun shined, the ocean answered. Watered every day. Spring into Summer, it got tall, taller, until a golden flower formed, shining like the headlight of a Lincoln Continental.

—4/28/24

JONES JR.
writing: Spring 2024

Illustration by Aaron Gunderson from
The Book of Ticks (2017)

Books by Good Deed Rain

Saint Lemonade, Allen Frost, 2014. Two novels illustrated by the author in the manner of the old Big Little Books.

Playground, Allen Frost, 2014. Poems collected from seven years of chapbooks.

Roosevelt, Allen Frost, 2015. A Pacific Northwest novel set in July, 1942, when a boy and a girl search for a missing elephant. Illustrated throughout by Fred Sodt.

5 Novels, Allen Frost, 2015. Novels written over five years, featuring circus giants, clockwork animals, detectives and time travelers.

The Sylvan Moore Show, Allen Frost, 2015. A short story omnibus of 193 stories written over 30 years.

Town in a Cloud, Allen Frost, 2015. A three part book of poetry, written during the Bellingham rainy seasons of fall, winter, and spring.

A Flutter of Birds Passing Through Heaven: A Tribute to Robert Sund, 2016. Edited by Allen Frost and Paul Piper. The story of a legendary Ish River poet & artist.

At the Edge of America, Allen Frost, 2016. Two novels in one book blend time travel in a mythical poetic America.

Lake Erie Submarine, Allen Frost, 2016. A two week vacation in Ohio inspired these poems, illustrated by the author.

and Light, Paul Piper, 2016. Poetry written over three years. Illustrated with watercolors by Penny Piper.

The Book of Ticks, Allen Frost, 2017. A giant collection of 8 mysterious adventures featuring Phil Ticks. Illustrated throughout by Aaron Gunderson.

I Can Only Imagine, Allen Frost, 2017. Five adventures of love and heartbreak dreamed in an imaginary world. Cover & color illustrations by Annabelle Barrett.

The Orphanage of Abandoned Teenagers, Allen Frost, 2017. A fictional guide for teens and their parents. Illustrated by the author.

In the Valley of Mystic Light: An Oral History of the Skagit Valley Arts Scene, 2017. A comprehensive illustrated tribute. Edited by Claire Swedberg & Rita Hupy.

Different Planet, Allen Frost, 2017. Four science fiction adventures: reincarnation, robots, talking animals, outer space and clones. Cover & illustrations by Laura Vasyutynska.

Go with the Flow: A Tribute to Clyde Sanborn, 2018. Edited by Allen Frost. The life and art of a timeless river poet. In beautiful living color!

Homeless Sutra, Allen Frost, 2018. Four stories: Sylvan Moore, a flying monk, a water salesman, and a guardian rabbit.

The Lake Walker, Allen Frost 2018. A little novel set in black and white like one of those old European movies about death and life.

A Hundred Dreams Ago, Allen Frost, 2018. A winter book of poetry and prose. Illustrated by Aaron Gunderson.

Almost Animals, Allen Frost, 2018. A collection of linked stories, thinking about what makes us animals.

The Robotic Age, Allen Frost, 2018. A vaudeville magician and his faithful robot track down ghosts. Illustrated throughout by Aaron Gunderson.

Kennedy, Allen Frost, 2018. This sequel to *Roosevelt* is a coming-of-age fable set during two weeks in 1962 in a mythical Kennedyland. Illustrated throughout by Fred Sodt.

Fable, Allen Frost, 2018. There's something going on in this country and I can best relate it in fable: the parable of the rabbits, a bedtime story, and the diary of our trip to Ohio.

Elbows & Knees: Essays & Plays, Allen Frost, 2018. A thrilling collection of writing about some of my favorite subjects, from B-movies to Brautigan.

The Last Paper Stars, Allen Frost 2019. A trip back in time to the 20 year old mind of Frankenstein, and two other worlds of the future.

Walt Amherst is Awake, Allen Frost, 2019. The dreamlife of an office worker. Illustrated throughout by Aaron Gunderson.

When You Smile You Let in Light, Allen Frost, 2019. An atomic love story written by a 23 year old.

Pinocchio in America, Allen Frost, 2019. After 82 years buried underground, Pinocchio returns to life behind a car repair shop in America.

Taking Her Sides on Immortality, Robert Huff, 2019. The long awaited poetry collection from a local, nationally renowned master of words.

Florida, Allen Frost, 2019. Three days in Florida turned into a book of sunshine inspired stories.

Blue Anthem Wailing, Allen Frost, 2019. My first novel written in college is an apocalyptic, Old Testament race through American shadows while Amelia Earhart flies overhead.

The Welfare Office, Allen Frost, 2019. The animals go in and out of the office, leaving these stories as footprints.

Island Air, Allen Frost, 2019. A detective novel featuring haiku, a lost library book and streetsongs.

Imaginary Someone, Allen Frost, 2020. A fictional memoir featuring 45 years of inspirations and obstacles in the life of a writer.

Violet of the Silent Movies, Allen Frost, 2020. A collection of starry-eyed short story poems, illustrated by the author.

The Tin Can Telephone, Allen Frost, 2020. A childhood memory novel set in 1975 Seattle, illustrated by author like a coloring book.

Heaven Crayon, Allen Frost, 2020. How the author's first book *Ohio Trio* would look if printed as a Big Little Book. Illustrated by the author.

Old Salt, Allen Frost, 2020. Authors of a fake novel get chased by tigers. Illustrations by the author.

A Field of Cabbages, Allen Frost, 2020. The sequel to *The Robotic Age* finds our heroes in a race against time to save Sunny Jim's ghost. Illustrated by Aaron Gunderson.

River Road, Allen Frost, 2020. A paperboy delivers the news to a ghost town. Illustrated by the author.

The Puttering Marvel, Allen Frost, 2021. Eleven short stories with illustrations by the author.

Something Bright, Allen Frost, 2021. 106 short story poems walking with you from winter into spring. Illustrated by the author.

The Trillium Witch, Allen Frost, 2021. A detective novel about witches in the Pacific Northwest rain. Illustrated by the author.

Cosmonaut, Allen Frost, 2021. Yuri Gagarin stars in this novel that follows his rocket landing in an American town. Midnight jazz, folk music, mystery and sorcery. Illustrated by the author.

Thriftstore Madonna, Allen Frost, 2021. 124 summer story poems. Illustrated by the author.

Half a Giraffe, Allen Frost, 2021. A magical novel about a counterfeiter and his unusual, beloved pet. Illustrated by the author.

Lexington Brown & The Pond Projector, Allen Frost, 2022. An underwater invention takes three friends through time. Illustrated by Aaron Gunderson.

The Robert Huck Museum, Allen Frost, 2022. The artist's life story told in photographs, woodcuts, paintings, prints and drawings.

Mrs. Magnusson & Friends, Allen Frost, 2022. A collection of 13 stories featuring mystery and magic and ginkgo leaves.

Magic Island, Allen Frost, 2022. There's a memory machine in this magic novel that takes us to college.

A Red Leaf Boat, Allen Frost, 2022. Inspired by Japan, this book of 142 poems is the result of walking in autumn.

Forest & Field, Allen Frost, 2022. 117 forest and field recordings made during the summer months, ending with a lullaby.

The Wires and Circuits of Earth, Allen Frost, 2022. 11 stories from a train station pulp magazine.

The Air Over Paris, Allen Frost, 2023. This novel reveals the truth about semi-sentient speedbumps from Mars.

Neptunalia, Allen Frost, 2023. A movie-novel for Neptune, featuring mystery in a Counterfeit Reality machine. Illustrated by Aaron Gunderson.

The Worrys, Allen Frost, 2023. A family of weasels look for a better life and get it. Illustrated by Tai Vugia.

American Mantra, Allen Frost, 2023. The future needs poetry to sleep at night. Only one man and one woman can save the world. Illustrated by Robert Huck.

One Drop in the Milky Way, Allen Frost, 2023. A novel about retiring, with a little help from a skeleton and Abraham Lincoln.

Follow Your Friend, Allen Frost, 2023. A collection of animals from sewn, stapled, and printed books spanning 34 years of writing.

Holograms from Mars, Allen Frost, 2024. Married Martians try to make do on Earth in this illustrated novel.

The Belateds, Allen Frost, 2024. The Belateds came to Seattle in 1964 and left the four chapters in this novel.

Jones Jr., Allen Frost, 2024. If you're a fan of 1970s television detectives, you'll be at home with this yarn.

Books by Bottom Dog Press

Ohio Trio, Allen Frost, 2001. Three short novels written in magic fields and small towns of Ohio. Reprinted as *Heaven Crayon* in 2020.

Bowl of Water, Allen Frost, 2004. Poetry. From the glass factory to when you wake up.

Another Life, Allen Frost, 2007. Poetry. From the last Ohio morning to the early bird.

Home Recordings, Allen Frost, 2009. Poetry. Dream machinery, filming Caruso, benign time travel.

The Mermaid Translation, Allen Frost, 2010. A bathysphere novel with Philip Marlowe.

Selected Correspondence of Kenneth Patchen, Edited by Larry Smith and Allen Frost, 2012. Amazing artist letters.

The Wonderful Stupid Man, Allen Frost, 2012. Short stories go from Aristotle's first car to the 500 dollar fool.

"I know darn well I can do without Broadway, but can Broadway do without me?"

—Jimmy Durante

www.ingramcontent.com/pod-product-compliance
Lightning Source LLC
LaVergne TN
LVHW031611060526
838201LV00065B/4815